LUST, LIES, & BETRAYAL

The Family Secret

PART I

LYNELL SMITH

Printed in the United States of America

Library of Congress Cataloging-in-Publication Data is available for this book.

LCCN: 2022950459

ISBN (Paperback): 979-8-9864237-0-8

ISBN (eBook): 979-8-9864237-2-2

First Edition: December 2022

Lynell Smith's books are available at special discounts for bulk purchases in the U.S. by corporations, institutions, and other organizations. For more information, please contact the Special Market Department at P.O. Box 831445 Ocala, Florida 34473, or e-mail lynellsmith@lynellbookstore.com

www.lynellbookstore.com

www.hopin2

DEDICATION

This book is dedicated to all individuals who have suffered some form of injustice; be it racism, sexism, gun violence, or domestic or sexual abuse. Do not allow the experience of your trauma to change your heart. Know that you're not alone. Continue to give the Universe the best version of who you are. It will take time to heal, so be patient with yourself and seek professional support if needed. Please don't dim your light due to adversity. Continue to shine. To be human means we must care for each other. There's an urgent need for our country to be more loving, respectful, compassionate, and forgiving. The moment we stop fighting for each other is the moment we lose our humanity.

Love,
Lynell Smith

TABLE OF CONTENTS

ACKNOWLEDGEMENTS

First, I would like to express my love and gratitude to my God for keeping me in the spirit, and for humbling me enough to make all of this possible. It is only through your grace and mercy that I have been able to accomplish everything in life.

Thank you to my readers for purchasing this book. Your support means the world to me and keeps me motivated to write more stories. So, thank you, thank you, and thank you!

A special thanks to my Developmental Editor, Black Lily Content Management, and Kye Bennett for supporting me on this amazing journey. To my two young sons, Dymere (Woody), and Milford (BJ), being your mother has inspired me to be a better person. The unconditional love you guys give me is unexplainable, and I am blessed to have y'all in my life as my sons.

TO THE READERS

If you are reading this book, it means you have invested in a good read - Thank you! A percentage of the proceeds from this book will go to Helping Other People In Need (HOP-IN 2), a not-for-profit 501c (3) tax-exempt organization. Forty percent of the proceeds will help to support the Safe Haven Home for sexually exploited youth. Your donations are the best way to help bring our vision to life. Below, you can find more information about the organization, how you can support it, and how you can get involved.

HOP-IN 2's mission is designed to reduce and prevent violence within our community by implementing programs teaching self-worth and by encouraging positive behavior, logic, and reasoning. We are driven by a single goal: to do our part to make the world a better place for all.

HOP-IN 2 will leave an impression on communities and people alike that will last an eternity.

www.hopin2.org
www.lynellbookstore.com

CHAPTER 1
Hell No!

It was a rainy Friday night. I had just arrived home from a 12-hour shift at Ta Soul Enterprise. 'Thank God It's Friday, the weekend romp was sure to be poppin', but I wasn't at all interested in clubbing. I hadn't been out in a while, and I had learned to accept it.

Fridays had become one of my best days because they offered me a golden reprieve; it was one of those rare days when I could truly relax without thinking about the stress of getting up early the next day for work. But it was clear my dwindling social life resulted from my job. Don't get me wrong, I absolutely love my job; it pays the bills, but it is definitely demanding.

I pulled off my long puffer coat and kicked off my shoes, reveling in relief. The coat was heavy, but it afforded me warmth, and more importantly, it was a significant piece of fashion. Walking off to the kitchen in search of a quick snack, I grabbed my mini radio, which was majestically placed on an insignificant piece of furniture I really didn't use for anything. I guessed it was probably the last place I'd had it when I jammed to it this morning. Call me old school or an old soul, but I loved the jam of oldies radio stations; they just knew how to select the songs to fit. Their playlists were just perfect.

Again, my stomach rumbled in protest, like it'd been doing for the past 10 minutes since I got home. I had been with a difficult client and hadn't eaten all day. I hadn't even remembered I was hungry until I walked into my house.

I moved towards the counter and was about to turn the radio on when I heard suspicious sounds coming from upstairs. My heart began racing as I stood still as a statue. Quietness persevered for a moment or two. I just stood still in the spot, frozen, listening for the sound again, but nothing. Then, suddenly, when I was almost settling in my mind it was nothing, I heard the sound again: *Bang. Bang.* Yup, there it is.

I immediately went into panic mode. I couldn't believe someone had the audacity to break into my damn house, a rush of adrenaline and a consequent surge of confidence followed that thought. Suddenly, panic was no longer my disposition. Oh, hell, no!

I grabbed my Glock .45 from the cabinet and proceeded towards the noise. I slowly crept down the hallway, trying not to be heard by the intruder. As I got closer to the sound, my heart raced, my hands became clammy, and sweat dripped down my face. As I wiped the sweat from my eyes, I remembered the survivor tip my dad told me when he taught me how to shoot, "Never let your enemy see you sweat."

Those powerful words are like an alcoholic getting liquid courage prior to being belligerent. I wiped my face one more time and instantly I felt my dad's spirit. The noise got louder and louder as I got closer. *BANG, BANG. BANG, BANG, BANG.* I kicked open the bedroom door with my gun aimed, loaded, and ready to fire. At that moment, I saw my life flash right before my eyes.

I was out of breath and tired but relieved to know the suspicious noise was from the window shutters I had forgotten to close last night. I was salty because I couldn't let loose on the trigger. The phone rang at the perfect time.

While running to answer it, I forgot I still had my weapon in my hand with the safety off. "Geez! That was a close one; I could have shot myself in the face," I stated while picking up the telephone.

"What was a close one?" a voice said on the other end of the phone.

"Hello! Who is this?"

"It's me, Monica. This is my husband's work line, but I'm calling you from it because I dropped my damn phone in the sink earlier, and now I need to get a new one. They ship it fast, though, so I should have it soon."

I didn't immediately answer. I was still trying to calm my breathing. I loved Monica, but sometimes she rambled on. At that moment, I couldn't care less about what happened to her phone.

"Whoa! What the hell is going on? You're breathing as if you just finished a marathon," Monica said, noticing my hard breathing.

"Girl, I thought there was a burglar in my house when I got home, and I was ready to shoot some ass, but it was a false alarm," I explained casually.

"I am glad to hear that, so what caused the confusion?" Monica asked.

She could be such a killjoy. Her responses would actually sometimes make you wonder what exactly went on in her head. I expected she would understand my situation and sympathize, but no, not even a little. Monica was just being Monica, commenting casually, without the slightest support. I sighed.

"Can you come over, and I'll explain everything when you get here? I could use a friend," I said dismissively, but not making it obvious. I needed my friend, and I knew she could comfort me, even though she was emotionally insensitive sometimes.

Monica hung up without acknowledging my request. For a moment, I wondered if it meant she wasn't coming through, but I quickly brushed the thought aside. Knowing Monica, she was probably on her way over, doing 90 miles per hour to be here as fast as she could. I checked the time. It was 7:00 p.m. I still had time to eat something, but the motivation for preparing something was long gone.

The events of earlier in the day had been outright disruptive, and now it was proving to be the end of my night. Still caught in the dilemma of an empty stomach, I persisted in reasoning a solution until a thought popped into my head. I quickly picked up my phone and texted Monica to get me something on her way over, most preferably a burger and French fries.

"I just hope she sees the text on time or even at all," I thought as I walked from the stairs, where I had been since the false alarm, downstairs in the sitting room, and laid on the couch, waiting for Monica's arrival. About 30 minutes later, Monica was knocking on my door, anxious to know what was going on. I watched her through the camera as she paced endlessly like she was being chased or followed or even stalked. Such a drama queen.

"Next time, don't take so damn long to open the door; now explain what had you discombobulated," she demanded in all seriousness.

"Did you see my text?" I responded, disregarding Monica's display of personality, eager to have some well-deserved food. Monica would always be Monica. Whether I was a second late or two minutes late, Monica would complain regardless. "Why are you looking at me like a mangled chicken? I said, did you get my text?" I repeated with a blank expression.

Monica just stared at me; I'm sure she was wondering how ungrateful my ass was being right now. I didn't mind, though; I was too famished to care.

"You bet I did," she finally said, laughing and handing me my takeout.

I opened the door properly for her to come in like she'd just handed me tickets to a live show. "Thank you, doll," I said as I hugged her.

"Oh, I see, so this was my ticket into your house," Monica joked while walking past me to the couch.

I burst into laughter as well, closing the door behind us. "First, I'm going to grab us a cold one from the refrigerator."

"Chile, your table is saying you had a cold one or two before I got here. This is ridiculous; you would think a man was here with these empty beer cans littered across this overpriced wood you call a table. Next time you want to pay $2,600 for some wood, call me and I'll cut down some of my oak trees from the yard and make you some furniture for a fraction of the cost. That high society furniture store you shop at saw a sucker coming through the doors, and that sucker was you," Monica stated, laughing callously.

I frowned. "You haven't been here five minutes and you're irritating me. We going to sit and chit-chat on the balcony," I responded, disregarding her comments. There was really no reason to get pissed; it was just Monica. It was a bad idea to let her know she'd gotten you angry because then the real drama usually started. Frankly, I'd rather avoid her drama.

"Now, I know you had too many damn drinks. Do you not see the rain? Better yet, do you not hear the thunder and see the lightning outside? Erica, your suggestion of sitting outside reminds me of when I was a kid and went to my grandmother's house in Florida. During the hurricane season, some Floridians threw hurricane parties. Only morons sit in the middle of a storm to barbecue and celebrate as if it was a sunny Fourth of July day," Monica said in her sarcastic tone.

So, I told her how the breeze and the sound of water soothed me, and she told me to take a shower and have a fan blow directly on me. She thought she was really funny.

"Well, the boom, boom, boom that sometimes sounds like an explosion, and that flash of lightning that shoots across the sky frightens me. When Mother Nature strikes the earth, I don't want to be nowhere around."

"Ugh! You are so extra, Monica."

"I'm not extra—I tell it like it is. Now, stop stalling and tell me what's going on with you, Erica."

I took a deep breath. "Well, ever since I took on this new business account at work, my life seems to have been upside down. My emotions are all over the place, and I'm hearing and seeing things that are not real. Do you remember a few weeks back when we went to the winery, and I had a bad feeling something was wrong but couldn't pinpoint the exact cause?" I questioned, waiting for a response before I continued.

"Yup, I remember," Monica replied.

She was really attentive, not making bad jokes or trying to interrupt me. She was committed to hearing me out as a true friend and sister. Those were the rare qualities of Monica and they were beautiful whenever they were on full display.

"Those same feelings are getting stronger and stronger. Tonight, was a prime example. I heard a noise and instantly turned into a gangster bitch. Monica, I am a peaceful person. I hate killing bugs, so why would I want to harm another human being?"

"Uhhh, because you thought someone was in your home, duh."

"No, Monica, it's not that simple to kill someone. The feeling I have is not a calm and collected emotion but an assertive, angry, combative, aggressive energy. Every little thing is ticking me off, which makes me become hostile as if I'm the female version of Dr. Jekyll and Mr. Hyde."

"Erica, you're feeling that way because when your Aunt Ruthie passed away, you stopped going to church and praying. Your soul is screaming to get in alignment with the Almighty God—that's the reason you have no peace," Monica cautioned and admonished at the same time.

Her comments were now inspiring some deep thoughts. At that moment, all I could basically think about were the many exhibitions of Aunt Ruthie's impeccable character.

"Funny you should say that," I said. "Yesterday, I was reminiscing about my Aunt Ruthie and how we had to attend Sunday Bible study early in the morning, followed by the afternoon services too," I remarked, smiling at the beauty of that memory.

"Don't forget Wednesday Bible study as well," Monica interjected.

"Damn, yup Monica, I forgot about Wednesday right after school at four o'clock. She had all the kids in the neighborhood come to her house as she preached from the Bible. The yardstick she kept in her hand meant all the children were on their best behavior, and she was not afraid to open a can of whoop ass on any hardheaded kid. Poor Jimmy, he was the only little boy who got beat with that stick. Do you remember that, Monica?"

"Yes, indeed! She beat him so bad he peed on himself and when he came to Bible study the following week, he was a changed boy."

We both laughed so hard, thinking about all the good ol' times.

Our prolonged laughter at the expense of young Jimmy was truly refreshing. Young Jimmy was really stubborn, but his stubbornness had been no match for Auntie Ruthie's whooping, and she did whoop him into some sense, eventually. Silence followed the preceding moments, with some chuckles, as we still relished the memory of Jimmy's troubles.

"Erica, it's getting late, so I need to get home before my husband starts tripping on me. If you lived closer and not in the boonies, I would stay longer," Monica eventually said, picking up her husband Anthony's work phone from the table, as well as her keys, ready to head for the door.

I should have been expecting that, after all, my house was in the boonies, but I truly didn't like the idea of Monica leaving.

"Girl, if you don't drop the dramatics—your controlling husband is not allowing you to stay out past 11:00 p.m.," I said, frustrated she was leaving.

Monica sat back down. My comment had obviously made an impression, considering the sad look she wore and the guilty tone she spoke with.

"Don't start, Erica. He's not controlling, just protective. Anyway, have you ever considered moving back to the city, so you aren't so far away?" Monica asked, trying to force a conversation, probably because of what I had just said.

"I'm not even going to answer that question, Monica. Thank you for coming," I said as I walked her to the door, and not letting her say another word. I needed to respect the fact she was married, and not be petty like some sad, single old lady. "Call me when you get home. I'm going to take a shower, so if I don't answer, leave a voice message. Hugs and kisses, girl, you know how we do."

We both chuckled at the roughness of Monica's lips when they touched my face and her spit rushed down my cheek.

"Once we got older, you would have thought you'd stop kissing my cheek like an elderly lady. Drive safely and call me."

Thank God that despite being drained, fatigued, overworked, and mentally exhausted, all was well. It was finally the end of my day. Right now, all I could think about was a nice warm bubble bath, so Calgon can take me away. The aroma of lavender permeated the air, soft lighting from the candles slowly danced across the walls in my master bath, and *Songbird* by Kenny G was playing sweetly through my multi-room audio system. With each garment I removed, I slipped out of the day's stress and released the burdens of my world as I stepped into the comfort of jacuzzi life.

*****

I tucked myself into my 1,500-thread-count Egyptian cotton sheets, which spread nicely on top of my California king-sized upholstery bed. My relaxed body sank deeper and deeper into the soft bliss of gentleness. The breeze on my face reminded me of the open window escapades from earlier in the night. I had forgotten to close the windows yet again. *"Argh Erica! My mind must be playing tricks on me,"* I thought as I slammed the stupid window shut! *"I hope I don't shoot myself next time."*

I chuckled at that line of thought, almost laughing out loud; it wasn't funny when it happened but replaying the experience in my head now seemed hilarious. I smiled again. Thank God nothing dangerous had happened. The tension I was feeling in my shoulders prompted me to stretch and turn.

As I readjusted back into a lying position and sank into the bed again, I thought about how far I'd come from a run-down one-bedroom apartment in the hood to this luxury home. I'd resolved the struggles I'd faced. Yes, there were inward scars and bruises, and frankly, I sometimes found it a little easier to cope now that I was mature. However, I found solace in the fact I hadn't turned into a fucking psychopath. As I reminisced about my teenage years, I was unsure if my feelings of reverie were good or bad since lately, I felt the trust of my own judgment escaping me.

I remembered school had just reopened in the fall, just after summer vacation. I was in ninth grade. It all began after school that fateful day. Science class was my last for the day, and although it was only just about to begin, all I could think about was the weekend; and the reason wasn't so far-fetched.

*****

Weekends were the most exciting for me because I got to spend my nights with Aunt Ruthie. Aunt Ruthie was simply the most amazing person in the world. Her heart was pure gold, and virtue was a quality she exemplified and modeled effortlessly. She taught me a lot of things about life.

You know how they say, "The environment you grew up in is what shapes the way you think?" It was true in my case.

Aunt Ruthie's environment contributed to many of my ideologies. She was 60-plus-years-old, but she had the figure of a 20-year-old woman. Every time I went out with her, young men would holler at her because she looked so young and vibrant. Women of her age were mostly insecure around her, especially when their husbands or boyfriends were present. Auntie's response was usually straightforward; she'd just chuckle and walk away. It was just in her personality to do so.

She didn't give two shits about who didn't like her. Her slogan was simple: "When you have a better opinion of yourself, you'll stop trying so desperately to get validation and approval from others. You'll be less needy, and more importantly, you'll find consistent inner stability, capable of withstanding the negativity the world propels and the uncertainness nature propagates." Yup! She repeatedly included this in the many lessons she taught me. And frankly, all those lessons had proven indispensable over the past years of my life.

Then there was my dad. My armor. *Mi amor.* He'd seen me through many hassles, and his unconditional care and protection towards me had been consistent since I became conscious of myself as a human being. He was simply the best dad ever. Sadly, he died a couple of years ago, but his spirit has been with me every day since. Anyway, between Aunt Ruthie and my dad, overall, I had a cultured upbringing. Dad was a traveling musician with his own band, so I attended countless sophisticated dinner parties and became well-versed in music and art. On the surface, I was set!

*****

"Erica!" the teacher screamed. "Do you not hear me talking to you?" he questioned, visibly frustrated.

"No, sorry, what did you ask?" The teacher's scream had snapped me back to reality, but I had veered off yet again. This time around, it was the pens in Mr. Ellis's shirt pocket; I mean, I just couldn't help but stare. *Why does he need so many pens in one shirt pocket? He must be a nerd; only nerds walk around like that.* Right amid my stare and thoughts, a pen burst right into his white-collar shirt.

"Mr. Ellis, you have blue ink coming out of your shirt pocket." I couldn't help but laugh as he excused himself to go to the restroom and clean up his nerdy, geeky self. The class erupted into organized chaos, as though we were all just patiently waiting for that momentary departure of Mr. Ellis. Typical ninth graders.

It was a defining moment of youth. The age of exploration. Ninth grade was the first year of high school and the craziest period of high school for most. Mr. Ellis was the perfect teacher; he understood us in a way that was amazing, and we truly appreciated him for that. But he was just too clumsy.

A male voice came over the intercom, interrupting the class. As though on cue, everyone went immediately back to their seats, listening attentively.

"This is Principal Watson. I have an announcement. If any of you would like to try out for the cheerleading squad, meet Ms. Shaw inside the girls' gym at three o'clock. School bus #480 will be 20 minutes late. Pick-up will be on the east side of the building. Remember, those who ride bus #480 will have a 20-minute delay, and all pickups will be on the east side of the building. Be careful as you travel home. Pay attention to your surroundings. I look forward to seeing every one of you at 8:00 a.m. Monday. Safe travels to your various destinations and have a great weekend!"

As soon as these late-in-the-day announcements began, I knew my last class for the day was almost over. Anyway, Mr. Ellis came back in time, just before the class ended, to apologize for any inconvenience he may have caused us. After apologizing, he then gave us weekend homework: "Read chapters five to nine and answer questions one to 40," he said.

"Nerdy ass teacher," I whispered under my breath. "Why does he always give us weekend homework? He's an idiot if he thinks I'm spending my weekend reading. Only suckers do weekend homework, you ass wipe." The whole assignment thing got me so pissed. You could see it all in my face, how angry I was while I walked out of his class when the bell rang.

Once I was out of the class, I walked to the girl's gym room at full throttle. I was nervous and excited at the same time. *You got this. Don't be scared. You are a Jackson, and we Jacksons are athletic and courageous. Hell, we are fighters.*

While I waited alongside the other girls already in the gym and those that had since arrived, an oversized lady turned up. At the sight of her size, the girl beside me and I looked at each other, perplexed. I whispered to her, "I hope this is not Ms. Shaw." We giggled quietly. Almost immediately, the lady started speaking, calling our attention.

"Hello students, I am Ms. Shaw. Today, you all will try out for cheerleading. On my command, do exactly as I say. If you fail to obey, you will be immediately disqualified and sent home. This squad is called the Dancing Eagles. Our colors are gold, green, and white, and we stand for academic, environmental, and relationship integrity. If you make the team, you will receive a booklet containing the Dancing Eagles introduction letter, the code of conduct, permission slips, our integrity slogan and its meaning, and finally, the community service rules and regulations forms. Being a Dancing Eagle requires discipline, time, and dedication.

"The Dancing Eagles are known for their outstanding team-building skills, community service projects, and competitions. When you girls step into this gym, I am your instructor, counselor, and friend. We are a team; without you, there's no me. Without me, there's no you. Please don't take my kindness as a weakness. Respect works both ways; you will respect me and me you. We have no time for bullying, horseplay, putting down, or embarrassing another Dancing Eagle. Any of these actions are unacceptable and will result in immediate disqualification. Three strikes and you are out. I take the Dancing Eagles very seriously. I have been its instructor for 15 years. Okay, okay, okay. Enough of all this serious talk. Let's get to the fun part."

Ms. Shaw then instructed each girl to grab a buddy. The girl who laughed with me earlier pointed at me, and I moved closer to her.

"Hi, my name is Erica Jackson."

"Hi, my name is Monica Johnson."

"Nice to meet you, Monica!"

Ms. Shaw screamed, "Now that you have your buddies, stand in two lines! I will demonstrate three cheerleading dance moves. First, a cartwheel and split, second, three flips and a split, and third, an eight-step dance count. Now girls, make sure you help your buddy as much as you can. When I'm done teaching you the steps, you'll have one hour to practice. Once the hour is complete, I will test you on your performance. This will include stiffness, team building, flexibility, and sound-offs. Are you ready!?"

"Yes!" we all screamed back.

"Get into two straight lines."

At those words, we immediately raced and formed lines with our buddies. When I got to Monica, she grabbed my hand. The moment that happened, I instantly knew we would become the best of friends. Ms. Shaw was just like the drill sergeant I was used to seeing in military movies. She was serious all the time. Her voice alone scared me, maybe because it sounded more like a male's than a female's. Then there was that little peach fuzz on her chin that scared me too. Yes, I was a kid, but I knew about body waxing.

She looked nothing like the cheerleader instructors I was used to seeing on TV. *Well, I will not judge how she looks; not everyone can look as good as Aunt Ruthie. Anyway, if I make the team, I will bring Auntie to my very first practice so she can meet Ms. Shaw.* She showed us the moves and did her thing. I would never have pegged her as someone that could lift her legs so high, and oh my goodness, her splits and flips were just amazing. *Oh man, I have to get on this team!* With every ounce of breath in my body, I wanted to be a Dancing Eagle.

The two girls in front of me and Monica were so scared and nervous. They failed the test when it was their turn to display exactly what they offered. Unfortunately, their intense nervousness cost them a spot on the team. Well, in all fairness, I thought they did an okay job. They would become better with practice. But Ms. Shaw wasn't having it.

"Sorry, ladies, you both didn't make the cut," she said. "Please grab your stuff and go home. Thank you for trying out and have a great weekend."

The sweat was already pouring off my forehead, my hands were clammy and wet, and my armpits were starting to stink. Nevertheless, my only focus was on making the team. As such, I didn't much care what I looked or smelled like. Monica and I were the next performers. Ms. Shaw called us, and we began our display. She counted every step Monica and I took. I stared into her hazel eyes as she counted, letting her know I was trying my best. *Pick me, please*! I inwardly screamed. It didn't take long for Monica and me to finish.

At first, Ms. Shaw just stared at us with a blank face; it was the longest 30 seconds ever before she spoke the most pleasant words. "Congratulations, ladies. Welcome to the Dancing Eagles. Pick up your booklets from the table by the wall; you girls may take your leave after that. Practice starts on Monday after school at the same time and in the same gym."

You would have thought I had won the lottery the way I jumped into Monica's arms. Even Monica looked surprised. At that time, I had never felt happier. I'd believed in myself, given it my best shot, and it had all panned out great. I was super proud of myself. I must admit, Auntie's affirmations helped me a lot; they constantly played over in my head, from the beginning of our display till the end. After picking our materials from the table, we shouted out together, "the Dancing Eagles are here!" and left the gym.

During our getting to know each other moments at the gym, Monica and I discovered we lived a couple of blocks away from each other. As such, when we finally were done with the whole exercise, just like we'd previously resolved, we walked home together. An unbreakable bond was formed that day.

My walk with Monica after school that fateful day remains the longest, I've ever had in my life. The school was a fair distance from our homes. It was in our neighborhood, but we were strolling as slow as the walking dead, unwilling for the conversation to end. We spent about three hours just slowly walking and talking. We wanted to talk about everything at that moment; get to know each other completely in one conversation. What can I say? We shared a special bond, and we'd been lucky enough to spot it early. The friendship we shared was rare; not many could boast of such a privilege. While we walked, we talked about virtually everything, from having single parents to everything else. Like myself, Monica was an only child with a single mother.

My house came first, so Monica and I hugged each other and bid goodbye once we got to my house. As I got into the house, I ran through the living room screaming, "Mommy!" in excitement. I was eager to share with my mom every detail of my very pleasant day at school.

However, after I called a couple of times and got no response, I opted to head upstairs. It was unusual for her not to respond. As such, with my school bag still in my hand, I just casually went upstairs, not to continue my search for mom, but to get ready for Aunt Ruthie's. I already knew Mom wasn't around; it was Friday.

The plan was simple: take a shower, pack them bags, and head over to Aunt Ruthie's. When I got to my room, I snatched my favorite towel off my bedpost and went off to the bathroom. As I turned the water on to fix the temperature, I heard a loud sound. Impulsively, I turned the water back off, paused for a second, and listened to see if I'd hear the sound again, but I didn't, so I turned the water back on.

However, while I was busy turning on the water, I glimpsed at my beautiful self in the mirror; that image stole my focus. I moved from fixing the temperature to looking my body over through the mirror. I noticed just how big my chest and butt were getting. However, it didn't take long for my focus to move from appreciating my natural endowments to the soreness I felt in my breasts from all the flips and jumps. *I have to ask Mom to get me a sports bra because these puppies are on fire.*

Still facing the mirror, I tried rubbing them to relieve the soreness, but it didn't work. Suddenly, I heard the same noise. I peeped out the bathroom door and yelled, "Who's there!?" but there was no response, just like before. This was the beginning of my nightmare. I decided to use the bath instead of the shower; I needed my body to soak to feel some relief. Of course, I knew there would be soreness. I mean, when has there ever been a workout without soreness, so I had prepped my mind for it.

But here's the thing; if tryouts could cause this level of soreness, how much more would an actual practice? After my bath, I headed back to my room to dry off and lotion up so I could get dressed and leave. I searched through my dresser, looking for underclothes to pack when I heard the noise again. I casually sought to find out what it was, and like many other times, I felt it was nothing, but I was wrong; this time was much different. As it so happened, immediately I turned to get the door, but it was pushed open.

A tall, masked man walked in from behind the door, grabbed me, and covered my mouth. He gripped me so tight I could barely breathe. Then he whispered in my ear, "Shut the fuck up right now." I started crying and screaming hysterically. He held me even tighter and mumbled, "Shut the hell up." I immediately stopped calling for help, but I couldn't help the panicking sounds; I was just too scared to be completely mute. To avoid looking at him, I fixed my eyes on the wall. "You're built really nice, just like a grown woman. I've been watching you; the way you throw your hair around, your pretty smile, and even the way you smell." He kissed and licked my cheeks. "You're a big girl now."

"Please don't hurt me," I whimpered under his palm.

"I'm not going to hurt you," he said, his voice callous.

My head turned as I tried to make sense of what was about to happen to me. *This can't be happening.* Who was he? What would he do to me? I tried but couldn't get a grip on my thoughts; they were running wild with all the possible outcomes. And each possibility bore fresh terror.

"Sir, please don't do this!" I pleaded. I don't know what I was expecting, but my desperation was beginning to sting, and anything to get me out of this had become a welcome resort. I don't think I was expecting he'd budge to my pleas, but I had to try something.

"Don't call me sir. Call me monster. Monster is what you'll call me."

His hot, stinky beer breath made me want to vomit. It dawned on me then that this was about to be a full-blown assault. If only I had my clothes on. This was the worst possible time to be surprised, moments after showering. It's the most vulnerable moment for anyone, and this stalker dude had taken advantage of it. I sighed inwardly yet was still in a panic. I wasn't giving up that easily.

"My mom will be home soon," I said, trying out another ploy to escape. I was hoping and praying this comment would scare him off. I was desperate to be free of this man; this monster of a human being, but my chances were looking bleaker with each passing second.

"No, she won't; she works late on Fridays. It's just the two of us alone in this big house," he said, laughing hysterically, not bothered in the slightest about my comment.

My antics had failed yet again. I was running short of ideas of what to do, and the situation was fast deteriorating.

He then snatched the towel off my body. I tried covering my nude body with my hands, but he pulled my hands over my head and started sucking on my breasts.

"Please, monster, don't do this," I pleaded hopelessly, crying in despair. Faced with the truth of utter powerlessness, I acknowledged there was nothing else I could do about the situation besides him choosing to stop.

He responded, "Shut the fuck up," pulled out a pocketknife, and threw me on my bed. He snickered and said, "I will slice your pretty face if you utter another word. Lay the fuck still."

Fear poured over me and I immediately went silent.

Monster touched all over my body. I was overwhelmed with utter terror, but I held back the tears and screams for fear of him killing me. After a while, I thought about cheerleading practice as an escape from the horror I was experiencing.

He stuck his hands in between my thighs and began to move up my legs. Eventually, he got to my privates. Then he spread my legs apart and stuck his finger inside me. "Are you a virgin?" he asked in between his moans. Well, regardless of his question, Monster didn't care or wait for a response; he just moved me up the bed and put his wet mouth on my vagina. With one hand, he held both of my hands, and with the other, unzipped his pants.

"Please don't hurt me," I begged. My heart was racing fast, and sweat was falling from my face.

He put his mouth back on my privates, and this time, he used his tongue. Afterward, he began kissing me. He kissed me so hard on the mouth, then thrust his penis inside me. It was the worst pain ever! His body began to move up and down on top of mine. He was breathing faster and faster. Blood was running down my legs, and my body was hurting even more. Still, Monster wouldn't stop; he did it faster and faster, harder and harder. No matter what I said, as I begged and whimpered in fear of him hurting me, he didn't listen. Regardless of my pleas, he just wouldn't budge. He continued until he was done.

As he climbed off me, he said, "You're a woman now. You're my woman now, and I can have you whenever I want. If you tell a soul, both you and your whole family are dead. I will kill y'all if you dare talk. I love me some fresh meat! You have no idea how long I have waited for you to develop a mature body. I get hard just looking at you. Now listen, I never want to see any boys around you; you belong to me. Just know that I'm watching you. Everywhere you go, I go, including cheerleading; you thought I wouldn't know about that, huh?" Then he laughed and left.

I lay naked on the bed where he'd left me, overwhelmed and drained, experiencing a weakness I couldn't quite explain. I cried. I just wanted to die. The ordeal felt surreal, and the real injuries were the ones my mind suffered, regardless of the pain I was feeling. The violence and horror that emanated from rape were things every young lady had read or been taught about, but none of us ever thought we would experience it. Yet here I was, now a victim, part of the statistics.

The thought of being part of a mass of victims gave me a strange motivation: I decided I wouldn't be another stereotype. Although I was gripped by fear and shame and badly needed comfort, I wouldn't tell my mom. I quickly resolved that she wouldn't be able to handle it; besides, she was far too unstable and fragile for such negative news and the guilt of not being home to protect me would cripple her for the rest of her life. I had to make this decision.

I struggled to sit up, grimacing in pain. The sheets were stained with blood. As I stared at the sheets, the reality of my situation dawned on me afresh. More tears rolled down my eyes. I accepted the pain and the shame and stood by my decision that no one would ever know. I cleaned the tears profusely falling down my cheeks and headed towards the bathroom, dragging the sheets with me. My perfect day had ended in the worst possible way.

CHAPTER 2
Just One of Those Days

———

"Ahhhh!" I screamed and jumped up from my bed. I was panting hard and all sweaty. "Phew! It's just another nightmare." After realizing it was just a nightmare, the alarm clock went off and began buzzing as though it'd been waiting for me all along. That aside, all I wanted to do now was hit the snooze button and go back to sleep. Nevertheless, I resolved to get up. I wonder if I'm the only adult still having dreams about being a teenager 20 years later.

Once I was up, I glimpsed at the time. *Time really flies by fast; it's 6:15 a.m. already.* I got my ass up and began prepping for the gym. *I have to get my body right and tight; maybe then, I can finally snatch up a man.* I brushed my hair into a ponytail. While I did, I realized my eyes were very puffy. I put some cucumbers on my eyes to help reduce the swelling; a beauty trick my auntie taught me. There was nothing cute or sexy about a woman who looked like she's been in the ring with Mike Tyson.

While I sat on the bathroom stool, waiting on the timer to buzz so I could take the cucumbers from off my eyes, I wondered if I'd eventually have to talk to a shrink. *Nope, that's out of the question.* The last thing I needed was to have my business splattered across the front page of a newspaper. The headline would probably read something like, "Successful traveling corporate marketing executive Erica Jackson just checked in to see a therapist." The writer would probably give it a little twist like, "She's getting the necessary help to ensure she is in the right state of mind when she gives her clients marketing ideas." Nevertheless, I would lose some of my clientele to such an article, no matter the twist. And I really couldn't afford to be losing clients now; I mean, I had to eat, and I needed a roof over my head.

Ugh! Today already feels like one of those days I end up feeling lethargic and joyless; Anyway, we will see. I got in my 2018 candy apple red Mercedes Maybach S650 Cabriolet and drove off to the gym. The sun was shining bright, and the smell of fall was in the air. The wind hit my face as I let down the windows. In a bid to enjoy even more of the fresh air, I let the drop-top down. To lighten my mood so that I can think happier thoughts, I put in a "Success Through a Positive Mental Attitude Motivational" CD by Napoleon. I engaged in a mind-training routine daily, playing motivational quotes while driving to the gym in the mornings.

The city should consider increasing the speed zone from 45 miles per hour to 75mph because whenever my foot hits the pedal, it's on and popping.

Ten minutes away from the damn gym, I got a freaking flat tire. *God damn it! What else can go wrong today?* I grabbed my cell phone out of my bag but quickly realized it had only a two percent charge left. *This cannot be happening to me; it's too early for all this bullshit. God, please, just send me help.* Owing to some misguided fantasy, a result of the many romance movies in my brain archives, I relished the thought that the man who stopped to change my tire would become my husband. *Maybe it's God's way of sending me the love of my life.*

Hahaha hahaha, who was I kidding? Mr. Right would probably never come. This had been my disposition forever. Not because I did not try, I did, but I just had the shittiest luck with men. One would think that after everything I'd been through with men I would have this proven phobia for a relationship, but uh-uh! That was certainly not my case. I guessed I was one of a kind.

Here was the thing, though; I didn't necessarily put myself out there, but I was open to dating, as long as whoever it was asked right. I'd usually oblige a date and see where it led. But so far, none had led anywhere reasonable, and now, after many successive terrible experiences, I was beginning to realize Mr. Right might just be a fairytale.

As I continued waiting for help on this lonely highway, another thought hit me. *I hope I don't become like one of those victims in a murder movie; a pretty girl deserted on the highway and murdered by a serial killer. Please don't let this happen to me. Pfffff. Come off it, that can't happen to you; moreover, I'm certain I don't fit the profile of a helpless, pretty lady.* Regardless of my bold self-affirmations, these thoughts got me rattled, and since I didn't have my Glock 45, I grabbed the mace spray in my purse and covertly placed it beside my seat, ready for any foolishness. I should have known something was off about today when I woke up with swollen eyes.

Still engulfed in these prevailing thoughts, a black Acura pulled up slowly behind my car. The sound of the engine immediately snapped me back to reality, and I observed the vehicle from my rear-view mirror. There was only one individual in the car, and it was a man. He flashed his lights to announce his presence, then turned off his engine and walked out. Instinctively, my arm moved to the mace as I watched him walk up to my window.

"Hello, Miss! I see your trunk is up with your hazard lights on. Maybe I can help?"

I stared hard into his deep blue eyes to see into his soul and decided I could trust him. "Yes, sir! I have a flat tire."

"You look uneasy; my name is Jack Myers."

No way in the world I was giving him my real name. "Hi Jack, I'm Nancy."

"A pretty name for a pretty lady such as yourself."

"Thank you!" I faked a blush, opened the door, and stepped away from the car so he could get to work. As I responded to his meaningless flattery, I thought, *Man, cut the chit-chat and change my damn tire*. This dude had absolutely no game; maybe a C for effort if I was being fair. Regardless of his obvious inexperience with women, he'd been the only one to stop and come to my aid. And I was not willing to lose him to any foolishness. It was compulsory that I be kind; at least until he was done changing my tire.

"I'll have you back on the road in 10 minutes."

"Okay, sounds great to me. I really appreciate you stopping and helping me."

"Not a problem! We all need help from one another at one point or another in life. I'm just glad I'm able to assist you in your time of need." Then he gave off a soft smile.

I smiled back. Ten minutes was beginning to seem an eternity because I really needed to pee.

"You are all done, Nancy. Here is my business card. And if you ever get a flat tire again, don't hesitate to call. Maybe we can discuss your tire problems over dinner and a glass of wine."

"Sounds wonderful! Thank you!" He gave me a warm massaging handshake, and though it felt comforting, it was unnecessary. "Thanks again. Do have a great day." After that, I stepped into my car.

But just before I drove off, he said, "You too. And I look forward to that phone call."

I laughed as I drove off. There was no way I'd be calling Mr. Belvedere or, better yet, Pillsbury dough boy to have dinner with. The man looked like he needed to put the donuts down and go on a diet. He was a hot ass mess!

By the time I arrived at the gym, I noticed my favorite parking spot had been taken. Ugh! I hated parking too far from the gym; anybody could break into your vehicle, and no one would see a damn thing.

As I stepped out of my car, I pushed the button twice to ensure my car alarm was properly engaged. I entered the gym and scanned my card, but it didn't work. Quite the day it was turning out to be. The attendant noticed my struggle and beckoned me to his desk. He told me not to worry about it, and that I should just write my name on the sign-in sheet.

When I walked away from the attendant, I noticed two ladies staring at me hard, but I just continued to the locker room. One of them eventually said, "Beautiful purse!" Without stopping for a chat or any form of pleasantries, I replied, "Thanks!" and continued with my journey. My face had now formed a big smile, and I was reminded once again why I loved the gym so much. It was not because of the superficial compliments that came from time to time. The gym was one of my best places because it offered me time and freedom to think while venting all my frustrations with the different workout machines available for use. And after the long week I'd just had, I sure had a lot to vent about.

Once in the locker room, I quickly changed into my workout gear and headed into the exercise area. I stepped on a new model treadmill as others were being used, and I waved at one of the trainers.

"Excuse me, sir, I'm having problems operating this machine. Can you show me what to do?" I asked Craig. He was the manager and our go-to guy for all difficulties faced with the workout machines. We'd known each other a couple of years now, but I had not lost the respect I had for him in the gym. He was the boss there, and I respected that.

"Absolutely! Oh! It's the treadmill. Okay, now my advice for beginners is to start your run at a slow pace. Maintain your pace for about 30 minutes, then once your body is in tune with the machine, gradually build up your speed."

"Thank you!"

"Enjoy your workout. And if you need further assistance, my name is Craig."

"Again, thank you!" I said, laughing under my breath and shaking my head. Craig never stopped surprising me and this time he was telling me his name like I was some newcomer. Well, he just loved to tease like that. It was his way of making you feel comfortable. Regardless of how long you'd been attending, a client was always a client, and a client was treated with utmost respect and attention every time. This is one of their codes of conduct, and they never fell short of living up to that standard.

"123 here we go, here we go, here we go, go, go, go, go step it up," a song blasted in my earbuds, hyping me up as I work out.

Time flies by quickly when you're having fun. I was on for an hour and a half, but it didn't seem like much time had passed. I only noticed when I took my earbuds out to listen to the lady standing in front of me.

When I was on the treadmill, I tended to just close my eyes and imagine I'm in the Olympics, running my heart out. With my Air Pods in, jamming to some hardcore rap music, my experience was always heavenly. My session usually ended when I was awarded the gold medal or something. It was funny, but it always gave me the extra push—the extra motivation I needed whenever I got tired. And over the years, it became a habit.

I had only noticed the odd lady standing in front of me when I opened my eyes after a successful stint. It seemed she wanted my attention, so I curiously took off one of my pods to find out exactly what she wanted.

"Erica Jackson, right?" the mystery lady asked very rudely. She had this arrogant aura, and it showed in the way she spoke. The way she was standing, with both hands on her hips, tapping her right foot repeatedly, got me even more curious. I waited for this encounter to unfold.

"Yes, and you are?" I replied sternly, not offering up any opportunity for her obvious foolishness.

"You don't remember me? You used to tease me in high school when we were on the cheerleading squad. It's me, Mariah Hughes," she finished, almost tauntingly. The audacity of this chick was something to see.

"Mariah, I remember your face, but the teasing part, I damn sure can't recollect."

I couldn't remember any Mariah in the cheerleading squad I was on, and considering we ran a pretty tight ship back then, it was impossible to forget a name. I might not have all their names at the tip of my tongue anymore, but if I heard any name from my squad, I was almost a hundred percent sure I would immediately recollect it. And aside from all that, I sure couldn't remember seeing such an ugly face in practice. I reckoned there wasn't anyone as ugly in my high school as the woman standing before me, rudely running her mouth.

"Let's go back down memory lane then," she sharply retorted. "It was you and the girl that followed you around everywhere. What's her name? Ummm yeah, Monica! The two of you made life hell for me in high school, and I will never forget the pain you caused me."

Stunned to silence, I stood perplexed at the accusation. Yes, it seems this woman knows exactly who I am, but it changes nothing. I don't know this person, and I am done playing nice. I am not about to entertain her foolishness any longer.

"Are you serious? We have grown up, and you're confronting me about some high school stuff that happened damn near 20 years ago?" I replied sternly, still trying my best to be calm and composed. I had learned to give people the benefit of the doubt, and I advocated for the same disposition among my peers. This was proving to be one of those moments I needed to practice what I preached. "You know what, I'll be the bigger person and apologize. I apologize for making your life hell in high school. Do you accept my apology?" I asked with subtle sarcasm. I couldn't help myself. Yes, I was being the bigger person, but even so, this girl was getting on my last nerves.

"Hell no! You and your apology can go to hell!" she screamed back.

"Well, I'm sorry you feel that way. Since you don't want an apology, you can build a bridge, cry a river, and get over it. I'm done with this conversation. You enjoy your day, Mariah," I blasted out at her, seeing I was dealing with an unreasonable child. I had no reason to be calm any longer. I knew her type, and they took your quietness as weakness. Call me whatever, but I was definitely not a sucker.

"Oh, it's not over. We'll definitely see each other again," she screamed again, fuming.

Good thing she'd kept her hands to herself, 'cause I was ready to brawl; her face looked like the perfect punching bag. "Are you threatening me?" I asked calmly, with a mocking laugh.

"I don't give out threats. I make promises, and I promise you we'll meet again," she responded arrogantly and started approaching me belligerently.

The gym instructor, who'd been watching from a corner, hoping for a peaceful resolution, quickly rushed towards us, eager to calm our agitation, seeing that a solution wasn't forthcoming. The club had an impeccable reputation, and the scene we were creating was bad for its image.

"Ladies, y'all have to leave the premises. The police are on their way," Craig sternly stated, standing between us to prevent the heated exchange from deteriorating into a physical altercation.

"Bitch, bye!" the mystery lady screamed, treading off angrily while making offensive signs with her fingers. She was truly crazy.

"You know what!? When you build that bridge and cry a river, jump in it instead and just die," I angrily spilled in response to her obscene gestures. This girl was being a real bitch, and at this point, I was being one right back! Even if she had problems with me, there were better ways to settle them. And to think it was all over some old high school drama? It was just insane.

I guess she wasn't ready for any hassle, the way she just up and left, not waiting for a further altercation. Craig was just being polite. He obviously wasn't asking me to leave, with me being a prime customer and all. But even I understood the plea would look biased if it was made to her alone. While we walked slowly and rhythmically toward the locker room, a conversation started. Craig, who seemed eager to know what the issue had been, quickly began.

"What happened? Why did she attack you?"

"Craig, it's a long story. Something about high school."

"Are you serious? This is unbelievable. I haven't really seen her here before. Hmm, people can be crazy," Craig stated matter-of-factly.

Craig lamented about some of the awkward run-ins he'd had with people throughout his life. I really cared little about what he was saying. He was being a bit extra and frankly it was pissing me off. But I just had to keep my cool. Not asking him to shut his damn mouth up was me being polite. That lady had put me off. I'd held my own pretty good, but I wasn't feeling it anymore.

My process had been disrupted, and all I wanted to do right now was just go home. The gym was supposed to be my zone, but the devil wouldn't just let me be. Craig continued speaking and rambling on incessantly. Phew! He only stopped after I tapped him on the shoulders after we got to the locker room.

"Someone broke into my locker, Craig. This can't be happening!" I lamented, infuriated, and frustrated at the same time, at the shitty turn of events. If I'd known this would be my experience, I would have just stayed home. All these hassles I was facing were just pissing me off even more.

Craig seemed to come back to his senses after my complaint. To me, he seemed like one of those guys that'd been single for a ridiculously extended period, which made them speak uncontrollably whenever in the company of a woman. You know, those guys that desperately want to share stories with any lady that gives them the slimmest of audience. In my opinion, that was loneliness, but most of them didn't listen, choosing to live in the despair of loneliness and in the beds of numerous partners, disturbing the peace of people when it was time for loneliness to collect a debt.

Craig examined the locker thoroughly, making sure the items I claimed were missing hadn't fallen down the side. They hadn't. I'd actually been burgled in broad daylight, and even worse, in a top-tier fitness center that was acclaimed as the best in the region.

"You can file a report once the police arrive here. Come to the front with me; I'll help you fill out an incident report," Craig advised, finishing his checks.

"Thank you; that would be helpful." Everything was in there: my purse, car and house keys, credit card, wallet, and money. "Shit," I lamented again, shaking my head in disbelief. The sound of approaching footsteps that turned into a man's voice halted my brewing rage.

"Someone call the cops?" was the next thing we heard from the mouth of a green-eyed, tall hunk of a guy in a blue uniform.

"Yes, my name is Craig, and I'm the gym manager. See that lady over there? Her purse was stolen from her locker."

"Hello, miss. I'm Officer Grenada, and this is Officer Beauford. Can you tell me your name and what happened?"

"I'm Erica Jackson. Well, it began in high school, apparently; but I'll tell you the short version."

As I gave my statement, I could see the expression of both officers change from interest to perplexity and then downright absurdity. Their final expressions could be interpreted as, "What the *=&%?"

"So, you're telling me this Mariah woman created this big scene over high school stuff?"

"Absolutely, Officer Grenada. I was just as perplexed when she approached me, yelling, and screaming; now, my things are missing. We searched the gym for Mariah, but she seems to have vanished. What's going to happen now?"

Officer Granada didn't immediately respond. He was making notes in his pocket notebook. It was clear he really knew the job. He'd calmed me down, and even I must admit that wasn't a simple thing to do, yet he'd achieved it effortlessly.

"First, we'll file a report, and then we'll look through the surveillance cameras. Hopefully, we will see who did this. We will pass your case to a detective for further investigation."

"No problem; I just want my car and house keys," I stated guardedly.

The two officers turned and were ready to walk away with Craig, probably to go review the surveillance tapes in his office, when Officer Beauford suddenly turned back and started speaking to me.

"Erica, be sure to call a locksmith to change your home locks; they can also make keys for your vehicle as well. Change your locks as soon as possible."

"Sure will, Officer Beauford."

The two officers proceeded with Craig inside. After about 10 minutes, they rejoined me in the locker room, where I was sitting, still disheveled.

"We can have the dispatcher send out a locksmith to make a key copy for your car, so you can at least get home." Thank you, Officer Beauford.

"Please do, Officer. I would appreciate it. I've had a really difficult day."

These officers were proving to be more than just life savers; they were decent human beings. I know they say the police are your friends, but 99 percent of the time, that isn't the case. Of course, there is the one percent, but it was very rare, and my experience with these fine gentlemen was one of those rare moments. They exemplified what an ideal police officer should be.

"Once the locksmith arrives, ask him if he can change the locks of your house. If yes, have him change all your house locks too," Officer Granada said, calling me back from my thoughts.

It is usually a delight to find something positive in every negative situation, and this was it for me, the kindness of these officers. "Thanks again, officers. You've been most helpful."

"Here is a copy of your report; it has our information and what transpired today. The case number is on it as well. A detective will contact you, but if you have any questions, any questions at all, don't hesitate to contact us. You be safe and try to enjoy the rest of the day, ma'am," Officer Granada finished, handing me the report.

"You, too. And be safe on the streets as well," I said, face down, keenly perusing the report they'd just handed me. This bunch was very thorough. The report was so finely written that it looked like I was reading from my memory.

"We will. Take care!" They responded and drove off.

Minutes after the cops left, the locksmith arrived. I'm glad he didn't take long because my patience was already running thin.

"Hello. I'm Erica, the lady in need of the key." I extended my hand out for a shake. The young man in front of me seemed to be kind; I suppose he was exactly the same way outside of work, but I was too eager for a solution to notice anything else.

"I'm Bob Russell. Nice to meet you, Erica," he said with a wide, radiant smile.

"A question, Bob, can you make a copy of my car keys, and once you're done, can you also follow me home so that you can change my house locks as well? And make duplicate keys? If yes, how much would be the price for both?" I got straight to the point. I had no time to waste. The way that lady was speaking to me earlier, how she made threats, I was right to be a little cautious and urgent with everything. I needed a solution as quickly as I could or I'd be in a seat of ruin, being piloted by some deranged woman.

"Let me get started with your car; I can quote you the price afterward. But both services will probably cost between $575 and $675. It all depends on the distance to your house," Bob stated casually.

"Bob, you're charging me almost $1,000 to change locks and copy keys! C'mon! And whatever you want to say now, we both know that amount is a bit steep," I interjected. I was stunned at the price he'd just mentioned.

"To be honest with you, the price would have been more; I'm giving you a discounted rate because of your situation," Bob explained.

"Okay, I appreciate the discount. Thank you. But everything is too expensive. Ugh!" I acknowledged, taken aback by his supposed gesture of kindness. Something was telling me he was right, and I wasn't about to rebuff my intuition, but regardless, the prize was just so high.

"Welcome to the adult world, Erica, where we are overworked, underpaid, and killed off by poisonous medication and foods," Bob added, shaking his head.

"You hit the nail right on the head, Bob." I snapped my fingers in jest, agreeing with his comment.

Bob took my response as an invitation to continue with his advocacy for the truth of the times we live in. I obliged him with further responses, and in the next couple of minutes, he'd raised issues that spanned several relevant economic, social, and health topics. But I could see he was being a conscientious listener when I spoke. He could talk, but he was finding it difficult to read my mood. Bob made a comment and an awkward silence followed, affording the both of us a moment of quiet. It was welcomed; I needed it because the prolonged conversation was getting on my nerves. I needed to get home.

"Sorry your things were stolen. I sincerely hope they find who did it," Bob said genuinely.

I'm sure he wasn't about to start another conversation because he could see the look on my face. I'd made it obvious just so he could notice. "Me too; she must pay." That was unplanned. I didn't mean for that thought to be audible. *Oh shit.* I immediately turned toward Bob to gauge his reaction. The way he was repositioning his body, I could tell he was about to give me a lecture. Oh! No! Here it comes. Those thoughts blasted loud in my mind as he motioned his mouth to speak.

"Don't seek or try to get revenge. Just allow the Almighty to handle it. Karma will surely meet up with her or the people responsible. There's no need to take matters into your hands; you'll only get yourself into trouble. Leave it to the cops and God; let them deal with those responsible," Bob finished.

Typical. I wasn't expecting anything less. I wasn't planning anything stupid either, like tracking down the woman and having her beaten mercilessly, but my ego wouldn't let me keep mute. I just had to say something.

"Where I'm from, once we find out who robbed us, we whip ass. If you're not careful, Ray Ray and dem might just whip their ass too," I said, laughing mischievously. It was normal slang in the hood, and Bob being White and all, I knew he wouldn't get the joke.

"Yeah, I understand. But who are Ray, Ray, and them?" Bob asked, evidently confused.

"'Ray Ray and dem' is slang; it is used to refer to the banding of family members and friends for ass-whipping endeavors," I explain, laughing even more.

"Wow, Ray Ray!" Bob said like he was still trying to make sense of the concept.

"Don't forget 'and dem'; that's a crucial phrase."

We burst out in laughter. Our laughter rang out for a second or two before I began speaking again.

"Well, Bob, you've learned new slang today," I said enthusiastically. I couldn't believe I was the one who couldn't wait for this conversation to be over a moment ago. Bob had somehow unraveled me with the way he spoke, his calmness, and his entire personality, so I was the one now spearheading the conversation. Whatever happened to my house and the urgency to get home? Phew!

"Agreed, but I don't know any Ray Rays, and I don't have any 'dems' in my family. So, I won't be needing to use this slang, ever," Bob interjected, chuckling freely. He was now relaxed while conversing with me and it showed in his features; the way he was smiling, his hand gestures, and the relaxed, consistent tapping of his foot as he spoke.

"Your wife must enjoy talking with you; you're so funny, and you're easy to converse with," I commented thoughtlessly, almost closing my mouth with my hands, afterward. For the second time in our considerably short conversation, I had spoken without caution.

"My wife died of cancer two years ago," Bob answered casually.

Damn! I didn't see that coming. "Oh! I'm sorry to hear that," I commented, shaking my head in disbelief and sadness. It truly was hard finding someone to love in this unstable world, where the vast majority live fake lives, and it was even harder losing love to such circumstances as death. "Did you two have any children together?" I asked, concerned, but even more confidently. Where was this boldness coming from, conversing with a total stranger when I had things to do? Sometimes, I surprised myself.

"No children together. But she had a son before we met, and I'm raising him as my own," Bob answered proudly. He steadied his eyes on the ceiling momentarily, like he was reminiscing about a fond memory, then shook his head and smiled.

"Amazing! You must be a wonderful man." I just had to say something to that. I mean, kindness didn't get better than raising a kid that wasn't yours.

"I started this locksmith business after she died; I needed another source of income," Bob continued, acknowledging my compliment with a big smile, but not commenting regardless.

"How old is your son? Sorry, my bad. I don't mean to pry into your personal life." I couldn't believe I'd been asking this nice, kind man personal questions, and I was only realizing I was prying into his personal life now. I could be quite the personality sometimes.

"Say no more. Are you ready to head home? I have another customer waiting," Bob responded sternly, yet smiling.

His smile was just effortless. I wondered how someone that had been through so much pain could smile the way he did.

"Yes!" I responded, both thankful the conversation had happened, and thankful it was all over. My mind had been doing marathons thinking about how to end the conversation but thank God he'd been the one to take the initiative.

"Give me your address. Let me put it in the GPS, just in case we split up," Bob advised.

Once I was done, he moved toward where his car was parked. He had been molding my car key while we conversed. Bob was parked just out front, owing to the fact that he'd arrived at the gym as quickly as he could after Officer Beauford called him. Officer Beauford was a friend of Bob's. I, on the other hand, had parked further down because my spot had been taken when I arrived at the gym earlier that morning.

As I approached my house, the feeling of paranoia set in; my heart started racing, sweat started falling from my face, and my hands became numb. *God, I haven't talked to you in a while. Please give me a hint or a sign about why I am paranoid.* These untamed, erratic emotions were driving me insane; one minute I was happy and the next moment I was not, as if I was having a panic attack. I hadn't even arrived home yet, but the overwhelming circumstances of my entire day to this point were doing a number on me. Then, to further compound my panic, I saw a black sedan with tinted windows speeding away from my house as I pulled up. *God, I am asking for your help, please.*

First, I looked in the rearview mirror to check if Bob was still following behind, but he wasn't. He'd been on a call while I was driving out of the gym. Otherwise, he should have been ahead of me, considering where I was parked. But I guess his call must have lasted much longer. I slowly pulled up to the driveway and remained in the car with all the doors locked. I was waiting for Bob to arrive before I made any move. This was new for me, Erica, depending on a man. Bob must have done quite the number on me.

While I waited for Bob to arrive, my front door suddenly flipped open. I didn't bother looking to find who it was. I just immediately dialed 911, put my car in reverse, and began speeding back to escape the intruder from my house. It happened so quickly; I didn't even see Bob coming up the driveway. Long story short, this resulted in an accident; my car had slammed right into his van.

"Fuck! Bob, are you okay?" I asked with concern, rushing out of my vehicle to check on him.

"Yes, I'm fine. What happened?"

"The cops are on their way. Someone broke into my house; that's why I was speeding backward," I explained, rattled, my voice noticeably shaky as a result.

"Erica, calm down. You're okay," Bob reassured, hugging me to calm me down. I was practically shaking. "Today is just not your day," Bob continued on a lighter note, seeing I had calmed a bit.

"No, it's not. And I think someone is after me," I insisted. I appreciated what Bob was trying to do; speaking on a lighter note, trying so much to calm me down, but the matter was way too serious for me to relax. I was absolutely unsettled.

I didn't really engage in anything that was too out there. For the most part, I maintained a focus on my job and my boring routines. I had a couple of projects here and there, but it was nothing too big, just mostly about the community. Plus, my job wasn't even high profile. I mean, I got paid very well, but I was a marketing executive, so who would want to hurt me? Yes, I had high-profile clients, but that wasn't a big deal; that was normal in my profession, especially if you were good at your craft.

Who was trying to hurt me? Was it still the same lady from the gym who claimed I had bullied her in school? Thoughts ran from one corner of my mind to another. I needed to know what was going on. Thank God the police were on their way; they would provide much-needed insight into my situation. I relaxed a little with that thought and just continued talking with Bob. Talking was helping my anxiety to calm.

While we talked, I suddenly heard a voice from behind us, "Get down on the ground." It was two police officers. They pointed their guns at Bob and me and screamed again in our faces, "Get the hell down now!"

I was confused by these instructions, so I still hadn't lowered myself to the ground by the time they reached us. The cops aggressively and forcefully slammed me down on the ground, while kicking and hitting me with their batons. I heard multiple voices screaming obscene words as I lay helplessly on the ground. I tried to get up, but a kick knocked the shit out of me.

Then I felt a boot hitting my face, and then blood dripped into my mouth. Every time I moved, it was reinforced that I should stay down with a hard stomp on my back. Never had I imagined being beaten in the street as if I was less than a human being, begging for my life and pleading with God to not allow me to die. I cried out for help and for them to stop, but my tears were in vain. Instead, the beatings kept coming blow after blow, so I tried to look out of my bloody eyes to see every officer who had taken part.

I noticed how nicely they helped Bob off the ground and began questioning him, leaving me to lie face down in a pool of blood. Right at that moment, I knew this had graduated from a simple response to a 911 call to racial injustice. Their actions and demeanor towards me were because of my skin color; they probably didn't imagine a

Black girl living in a White neighborhood such as this. I was reminded of the incident from all those years ago. I couldn't defend myself then, and I still couldn't defend myself now. I felt powerless. I must be really unlucky because over the course of my short time on earth, I had become accustomed to pain.

I blacked out for several minutes, but I heard Bob yelling at the officers, "What are you guys doing? What is your fucking problem? You can't treat people like this," Bob commanded. The way he was standing beside the officer who had me pinned on the ground, screaming, was a sign he would have shoved the officer off if he wasn't being cautious. Bob immediately picked me up, seeing the officer had retreated from his hold on me. Bob kept screaming out my name, but I was dazed due to the impact of my head hitting the pavement.

"She's bleeding. She needs an ambulance. Call the damn ambulance now, or I will see your ass rot in hell," Bob barked at the officers.

It would seem Bob was a popular figure, or maybe it was just God's intervention because they did all he asked and left me alone to call the ambulance.

"It's going to be okay. The ambulance is on its way." While Bob talked, he wrapped me in his jacket and tried wiping the blood from my mouth, ears, and face, but the blood kept coming.

"I can't believe I was just the victim of racial injustice; this is insane."

"I'm here with you, okay? I'm not leaving you," Bob reiterated, but I was already out cold.

I couldn't have thanked God enough that our paths chose to cross on a day as horrific as the one I was experiencing. His appearance had been timely, to say the least, and his being with me through this ordeal helped me deal with the pain and the reality of the situation I was facing.

As I regained consciousness, my eyes were welcomed by a white roof. Then I started hearing different beeping sounds, and it clicked. *Woah! I'm in a hospital! Wait, remind me how I got here.*

"Good morning, Ms. Jackson. Do you know where you are?"

"Yes. I'm in the hospital," I answered confidently. It was all coming back to me, the push from the back, the smack of my head on the pavement. "Ahhh," I grimaced in pain. The pain in my head rushed back with that thought, and I was forced to feel my head, a response to stimuli.

"Great, I'm Nurse Bennett, and you are at Smithville Medical Center. Do you remember how you got here?"

"No!" I said, in shock and confusion.

"An ambulance brought you here yesterday afternoon. We were told police officers assaulted you. You were bleeding from the head, mouth, and ears when we admitted you. We took a full CT scan to get complete imagery of your head and body so we could check if you had a brain injury and any form of broken bones. The scan showed that you have a concussion, a sprained arm, and a broken eye socket. You'll be on bed rest for another day or two so the doctor can monitor your vitals. You'll be discharged when you're stable. By the way, you had a few visitors this morning; a man named Bob and two detectives. The detectives left their card on the nightstand next to your bed."

"Thank you so much, Nurse Bennett." I managed to muster a smile as I spoke.

"Rest up, and if you need anything, just push this button here."

"Alright. Thank you once again, Nurse."

Moments after the nurse left, I heard two knocks on the door. I watched as the door slowly opened. Then I hear a soft, deep, Denzel Washington-like voice say, "Good afternoon! How are you feeling?"

Oh! It's Bob. "Hey, Bob. Not too good. I'm in a lot of pain."

"I bought these flowers for you."

"Thanks, they are beautiful. You can sit them on the window ledge."

"I've changed all your locks, and I fixed the broken window too."

"There was a broken window too?" As I repeated his words, my heart dropped. "Who would do something like this? If it's the lady from the gym, then this has gone beyond a high school feud."

"Don't you worry your pretty little head; I've taken care of everything. I also took pictures of all that was vandalized for insurance. Then I filed a police report on your behalf."

"Bob, I appreciate all that you've done. How can I return the favor?"

"You can return the favor by healing and taking care of yourself. You've gone through a lot, and I feel it's my job to assist someone who requires help. Heal so you can sue the pants off those racist bigots. My advice is to get an excellent, out-of-state attorney who specializes in police brutality. Find someone that got licensed in Atlanta. Also, don't entertain interviews with the cops or the press if the subject of their interview is about or around the assault. Don't talk about the incident until you're ready to sue. I can tell you this much, anything you say to the cops, or the press now will be used against you later. So, you just rest up and get better and I will be on my way, and you can get your much-needed rest."

"No. You can stay if you wish. I enjoy your company."

"I would love to, but I have a few more customers to service. But if you like, I can come back when I'm done."

"I would love that."

"See you later then. Get some rest. And remember, talk to no one."

A few hours after Bob left, Nurse Bennett entered the room and began, "Excuse me. Miss Jackson, you have two visitors."

"Hi, Miss Jackson. I'm Detective Ramon, and this is Detective Forgo."

"Sorry, detectives, I have nothing to say. Please leave my room."

"But Miss Jackson, we would like to ask you a few questions; we are here to help."

"Leave my room now!" I screamed at the top of my lungs.

Nurse Bennett ran back into the room. "Alright, detectives, it's time for you to leave; she needs her rest now."

"When you rest up, call us; you already have our card."

Once the detectives left, I called back the nurse.

"Nurse Bennett, please, I want no more visitors other than Bob. He is to be my one and only visitor. Can you make that happen?"

"Will do! And dinner will be served soon. You were sleeping when I placed the dinner order, but you can change it if you desire."

"No, it's okay; I'll eat whatever you ordered."

"It's mashed potatoes and gravy, meatloaf, green beans, dinner roll, and jello."

Bob sure better come soon before they poison me with this jailhouse food. At that thought, I felt a thrust of pain. The little smile that was beginning to form disappeared, and the pain dragged me into a state of dysphoria. Before long, I began to cry. *Why is all this happening to me?* I felt distraught, and I was in severe pain. But there wasn't much I could do but cry, and I just continued crying until I fell asleep.

I just needed to make a full recovery so I could finally leave this damn hospital. And that question of "what else can go wrong?" was one I was never asking again in this lifetime. The universe had a way of showing you just that.

LYNELL SMITH

CHAPTER 3
Unforgivable

It was finally Tuesday, the day of my discharge from the hospital. I was excited to be leaving. I could finally have some decent, home-cooked meals. If not for Bob's constant prompt intervention, I would have been at the mercy of the hospital's jail food. But still, I was tired of all the take-outs. I desperately needed a home-cooked meal. *Bob*.

His name rang in my mind for a long second, and I began smiling sheepishly. Bob, a total stranger who was only supposed to fix my locks, had ended up fixing other things. He had been the one taking care of me and my business all the while I'd been in the hospital. I was eternally grateful. I was actually shocked at how I'd allowed myself to be helped by a man, especially a man I didn't know all that well. *Miracles do happen, I guess*. In fact, I had grown so accustomed to Bob that I couldn't wait to see him.

The sudden creak of the door called my attention, breaking me out from a trend of welcoming thoughts. I turned to see who it was; it was the nurse. I shook my head and scoffed. I was really hoping it would be Bob.

"Miss Jackson. Would you like a cab voucher?" Nurse Bennett asked from the hallway, holding the handle of the door to my room.

"No thanks. My friend is coming to get me," I answered, smiling.

The nurse motioned into the room following my answer, sure she didn't need to make any arrangements. Nurse Bennett stopped in front of me, handing me some papers.

"Okay. Just sign here. These are your discharge papers; I will make a copy for you, then you are free to leave," she said with a smile.

I couldn't have asked for a better nurse. Her bedside manner was the best that anyone confined to a hospital bed could hope for. She'd been amazing. She quickly used the photocopier and made me a copy.

"Here you go, miss. You're free to go," Nurse Bennett said, handing me the papers a second time around.

I received them and smiled at her. "Thank you for all your help. And do have a great day."

"You as well. Best wishes with everything!"

As the nurse walked out, my mind wandered about how corrupted the police department and justice system are. The time in the hospital, with the incident and all, had really offered me some much-needed perspective. The incident with the police was a sad one, but it dawned on me afterward that I wasn't really living life, I was just going through it, and all that had to change. When your life flashes through your eyes like that, and you survive, it feels like you've been given a second chance to do things much better. Of course, the debacle with the cops was somewhere in the corner of my mind, but frankly, I hadn't really given any thought to pressing charges and all the other hassles that came with it. I just wanted to first take time and heal, then go from there.

The door creaked. I didn't bother looking; I was sure it was Bob. I just picked up my phone from behind me, ready to leave. The door opened, and it was Bob. I thought as much. He walked in, got my stuff, and we walked together to his truck. When I was finally seated in his truck, I breathed in the fresh, natural air I'd missed for what seemed like an eternity.

"Bob, I can't wait until I get home to fix me a home-cooked meal," I said excitedly. I could already see the combination of food I was going to eat. It was just three days I spent in the hospital, but it felt much longer.

"Erica, what you need is rest," Bob interjected, with a serious look on his face. This young man was talking to me like he was my husband. And although that was all cute, it could be perceived as offensive as well.

"What I need is a good bath and some food," I replied, ignoring the tone of his comment.

Bob gave me a weird look and then began with his plea. "We haven't known each other long, but I already feel like I've known you for a long time. Would you mind staying at my place? Just until your injuries fully heal. I would feel much better knowing you are safe, considering that whoever broke into your house could make another attempt."

"Bob, you have done so much. I still owe you for the changed locks—"

"Erica, you owe me nothing; it's on the house," Bob said, smiling and cutting me off.

"I'm not even the slightest worried that they'd try another attempt; my instincts say they won't. Right now, I have bigger fish to fry; you know, like finding a lawyer." This comment was unplanned. I wasn't even thinking about all that now. But somehow, Bob had forced the comment out of my mouth. This was how you knew a conversation was getting on your nerves.

"Yes, speaking of that, I found some out-of-state lawyers online. I reached out to a few while you were still in the hospital," Bob responded casually.

What the? Okay, I'm done. I'm done pretending this is normal. What's with the overt display of care? I mean, I just met the dude, and he needs to take a chill pill. "Bob, I know you want to help and all, but the way you are taking this, it feels like we are already in a relationship," I cautioned.

"I am not acting like we are in a relationship; I am just acting the way a man should treat a woman who needs help but is too proud to ask," Bob interjected, still smiling calmly like he had me all figured out.

I eyed him in contempt; I didn't want him to know what I was thinking, and I didn't want him to feel like I had lost my cool. I didn't have many options or else I would have had him pull over so I could be out of his vehicle because he was seriously getting on my nerves. "Alright," I shrugged, admitting defeat. "Let me think about it. And don't forget, you aren't living alone. You live with your son; I really wouldn't want to impose on his space," I responded, keeping my cool, and at the same time touching on a sensitive topic to gauge his reaction.

"Can you let me know by tomorrow night, so I'll know if I need to make further preparations?" Bob questioned in response. The smile was off his face now. That wasn't a bad response; it seemed to be the response of a man who was resolute about what he wanted.

"Sure." Thank God all that was over.

As Bob pulled up the driveway, my mind traveled back to the event that occurred here some days back. The horror of the incident played back. For a moment or two, I was frozen right where I was seated, in the front passenger seat, completely still, like I'd seen a ghost.

"Are you okay? You zoned out for a minute?" Bob asked with concern, the look of worry adorning his face.

"Actually, as you pulled into the driveway, I had flashbacks from the other day," I explained, still rattled.

"You see; therefore, you need someone around. A friend must stay over with you, or you need to stay over at a friend's. Staying here, all alone, is only going to get you more rattled."

What? This dude didn't know when to stop. "Please stop with all that. I can take care of myself. I don't need anyone to take care of me," I replied, pissed at his insistence on that subject. I wasn't handicapped or anything. PTSD after such an incident was absolutely normal. PTSD didn't mean I now needed help with living. Damn!

"You women with your 'I'm independent and don't need nobody attitude' really get on my last nerve," Bob responded, laughing awkwardly.

I turned to look at him, eyeing him with contempt. That was it. The audacity! There was no way this conversation was going to continue after that comment.

"This conversation is over, Bob. I need to rest. Thanks again for dropping me off. I will call you tomorrow." I stepped out of his truck and shut the door behind me.

Just then, my phone began ringing. Thank you, God! It couldn't have rung at a better time as I really couldn't deal with the eye contact about to ensue before going into the house. I picked up the phone and began walking towards my door. Bob took the cue and drove off. I couldn't tell if he'd driven off pissed at my response, but whatever, I didn't care. He'd crossed a boundary he should have been sensitive enough to maintain. All that talk about women doing this and that was bullshit. Men and their stupid egos. You would rather ruin a beautiful, budding friendship than simply take a no? I was fuming. The whole thing was totally messed up, and it'd gotten on my nerves so much. Even after I tried dismissing this talk earlier, he kept going.

"Where the hell have you been? I've been calling your cell and house phone, and every single time I've called, it goes to voicemail. We even stopped by, but we found no trace of you."

"Monica, I was at Smithville Medical Center," I replied forcefully, almost arrogantly. I wasn't in the mood for any kind of confrontation, no matter the reason, thanks to Bob.

"What?! Wait, why?" Monica asked.

She seemed not to have picked up my tone. I guess what I had just said was more shocking. Whatever the case, her reaction had calmed me, because I was ready to bring it after my fallout with Bob. Maybe I had been too harsh with him. Bob had been the only one with me throughout this ordeal, and he didn't deserve to be spoken to the way I did. I made a mental note to apologize to him later.

"Long story. Someone stole my purse at the gym on Saturday. When I arrived home, I noticed the front door was wide open. Someone broke into my home. Subsequently, I called the police. However, they assumed I was the burglar and slammed me hard to the ground when they arrived. Now I have a concussion, sprained wrist, and a broken eye socket," I explained.

If anyone could understand the problem and experience of police brutality, it was Monica. We'd grown up in the same neighborhood and we'd witnessed countless times what the police did to young men and women of color. They attacked people of color for no reason. The situation was so bad that almost every Black person had a mutual person or relation that had experienced police brutality, racial injustice, and so on. Black people are profiled, period! We are labeled as what we are not, and our deaths are explained away with the most ridiculous logic.

"Oh, my goodness!" Monica exclaimed, stunned at the news. Silence followed her display of shock. Her breaths were now long and deep, but she still said nothing.

Even though she distanced the phone from her ear, I could still hear her voice in the background, and I could tell from her voice that she was about to cry. Monica was the emotional type. She was resilient and not a lady to mess with; simply put, she was a lady that could hold her own in an argument or anything at all, but she also had this totally soft side and a very compassionate heart. News like what I had just shared always broke her heart.

"Monica, don't you dare start with your crying; you're going to make me cry too," I emphasized. Monica's shaky voice in the background abruptly detracted, followed by brief, periodic sniffing.

"Erica, I'll be there in 15 minutes," Monica replied, her voice much more stable now as she disregarded my comment.

It seemed she'd gotten a grip on herself, probably for my sake. We shared personality similarities. Like Monica, it was usually difficult for me to stop whenever I started crying. I guess she was somewhere nearby because her house was much farther than 15 minutes. But I was grateful she was close, and more importantly, she was coming over, because the thought of negative probabilities was beginning to haunt me.

While I patiently waited for my best friend, I poured two glasses of my most expensive wine. It was $3,000 a bottle. Hopefully, I could drink away my scars and pain. All my resolutions about life while in the hospital were becoming a distant memory. I guess the idea of stability, and Bob handling my business while I was handicapped, contributed to those resolutions because now I couldn't care less.

Really, it was true; this house was truly too big for just one person. I thought I should move into my small private cabin in Hooperville County.

Monica arrived and went crazy banging at the door my door like she was the cops. I knew it was Monica immediately when the bang on the door was repeated. I wasn't surprised; I think she'd made a pact with herself that she would always announce her presence with so much nuisance. I guess in her mind it was more notoriety than a nuisance. Typical Monica.

"Hello, sis. You got me out here knocking in the dark while you got yourself a stalker lurking around," Monica joked as I opened the door.

"Ha, ha, ha, not funny, Monica! Get your ass in here before you stay outside permanently," I replied, dragging Monica inside rapidly, into a hug. It was just what I needed at that moment.

"It's okay. It's okay," Monica comforted me, patting me on the back lovingly. Then she pulled me away from the hug to look at my face properly. "Look at what those bastards did to your face. Tell me everything; don't leave anything out," Monica continued, examining my face thoroughly.

That was something I hadn't thought about: my face. I hoped I didn't look too ugly. "Come to the family room; I poured us a glass of Coche-Dury Corton-Charlemagne Grand Cru," I interrupted, shifting my head away from the meaningless examination. She wasn't a doctor or anything, she was just being herself. And frankly, I was just tired of tilting my head from one side to the other for Doctor Monica.

"What the hell is that?"

"It's wine, Monica."

"Give me the regular wine with a name I can pronounce; not that bougie shit you are drinking."

"Ugh, I can't win with you! This wine was imported from France."

"Exactly! Bougie!"

"Drink the damn wine and be grateful. I never thought I would ever be a victim of police brutality; I would never have imagined I could be humiliated and mistreated because of the color of my skin. The news is everywhere; on TV and the radio as well." In the middle of my lament, I broke down in tears.

"Erica, we colored people experience these problems every day. Stop crying; it will all be okay!"

"No, it won't; look at my face. Look at my body."

With every tear, I got angrier, and the thought of revenge further boiled within me. I was overwhelmed with hurt, embarrassment, and disappointment. In a bid to gain comfort, I lay in my best friend's arms and cried till I fell asleep.

"Good morning, rise and shine!"

"Damn! Monica, stop yelling. And what time is that you're waking me up this early?"

"It's 11:30 a.m., Erica. I cooked you breakfast. Get washed, then come downstairs so you can eat."

"I can't move; my head hurts."

"It should. You drank the whole bottle of that Bougie nasty-ass wine last night."

"No! Not the whole bottle?"

"Yes, Erica. The whole damn bottle."

"That's a $3,000 bottle."

"Girl, have you lost your everlasting mind? Who do you think you are, Oprah!?"

"Stop screaming, Monica. Seriously, please stop. I have a headache, and the sound of your voice is annoying. Let me go take a shower; I'll be down in a few."

"I can bring the food upstairs if you prefer."

"No, I'll come down. Thanks for everything."

As I examined the bruises on my body with a puzzled look, I vowed never to let another man humiliate or mistreat me ever again.

"Every cop that hurt me will pay; I promise! You will pay!"

"Erica, are you okay?" Monica asked. There was so much worry in her voice.

I ignored her.

"Erica, who are you talking to? Erica!"

I intentionally drowned out Monica's voice until it finally faded away. After about 10 minutes of meditating and calming the inferno burning within me, I finally came out. Monica had left the room; I guess she got tired of getting no response. I walked down to the living room, where Monica was sitting.

"About time you came out of the bathroom; your food is already getting cold. And a man named Bob called while you were in the shower."

"Thanks."

"Are you okay? I am worried about you; you look spaced out."

"I'm fine. But you can go home now. As a matter of fact, I have some errands to run today."

"Well, I can go with you."

"I don't think you need to. You should go home to your family. Your husband misses you. Go home to him."

"I don't like the way you're talking. Your tone frightens me. You sure you're okay?"

"If you ask me that question one more damn time, I'll snatch out your tongue from your mouth and wrap it around your neck."

"Erica, I'm gone. You are tripping."

"Let me walk you out to make sure the door is locked and all."

When she got to the door, she turned with a worried expression on her face. "Call me later, Erica. I'm perturbed about your sudden change of attitude."

Although my response was a smile, inwardly I rolled my eyes. "There are a lot of things on my mind right now. Plus, I would like to focus on the important stuff without being disturbed."

"Okay, just be good, right?"

"Sure. Have yourself a great day. Bye!"

Once she turned to leave, I shut the door with a sigh of relief. Monica could be irritatingly kind. The first thing on my to-do list was to get me another bottle of wine.

"Where is my damn cell phone? Drew, locate my phone." Drew was my house's AI.

"Drew is locating your phone now."

Thank God for technology. If it weren't for Drew, I would have to buy a new phone every month.

"We found your phone. It is inside your pocketbook." Great! I can order a bottle before I leave the house

"Good morning, Vanessa," who's my boss's secretary, "This is Erica Jackson. The phone is breaking up. Can you hear me?"

"Yes, I can hear you."

"Very good. Can you please send me to Dr. Wang Wei's answering machine?"

"Yes, I can. But would you also like me to take the message?"

"No thanks. I'd prefer to leave a voicemail instead. It's quite urgent."

"Unfortunately, Dr. Wang Wei is on a two-week vacation, and all voice messages will be answered once he is back in the office. However, he said I could contact him, but only in case of an emergency. I have his direct contact number for that purpose."

"Vanessa, it's an emergency."

"Okay, I will inform him. He will return your call at his earliest convenience."

"Thank you. Do have a great day!"

"You too. Bye!"

Dr. Wang is going to be so pissed when I give him the bad news. My life is so out of control. God, please give me the strength to deal with this situation.

Father God, please answer my prayers because I don't know what to do or where to go! Nothing is going right for me. I know I've made plenty of mistakes, but I did nothing bad enough to deserve what is happening to me now. Dr. Wang has a cold heart; please don't allow him to take all my business accounts away from me and give them to someone else, because if this happens, I will have to seek employment elsewhere.

As I finished my prayer, I recalled my argument with Bob. Maybe I was too harsh? As though on cue, my phone rang, and it was Bob.

"Bob, you must be psychic; I was just thinking about you, and then you rang."

"Hopefully they were wonderful thoughts."

"I wanted to take you up on your offer to come to stay with you at your house."

"Well, I'm delighted that you have decided to say yes, and I can't wait to see you! What day and time can I expect your arrival?"

"Well, I'll start getting ready once you give me the address."

"Alright, I'll text it to you."

"Thanks, Bob! I'll see you when I see you."

"Drive safe, Erica."

He hung up and I ran off to prepare. Once I had my things packed, I walked to my front door. Before I stepped out of the house, I turned to give it one last look. I was definitely not going to miss the loneliness I had experienced here. Then I opened the door and walked out, straight to my car. I put my bags in the trunk, fed the GPS the address, and then I was off. After 15 minutes, I noticed a vehicle had been behind me at every turn. In still calmness, I connected my phone to the Bluetooth and called Bob hands-free; I didn't want my stalker to notice I was on to them.

"Hello."

"Bob, I believe I'm being followed."

"Don't panic. Use your rearview mirror to observe. Now, tell me what you see."

"A black car with tinted windows is behind me."

"Are you sure?"

"Yes. It's been on my every turn since I turned off my street. But here's the thing, the car behind me is moving slowly, so now I'm unsure if whoever it is, is really on my tail or not."

"Erica, you might be a little paranoid because of the incident that occurred last week."

"Yeah, you may be right. I'm tripping."

"It might be an old person driving Miss Daisy."

"Who's Miss Daisy?"

"You don't know the movie where Morgan Freeman is the chauffeur? Or you don't remember seeing it? Which is it?"

"I really can't recall."

"Hahaha, you've got to step up your movie game. That movie is a classic; everybody has seen that movie."

"Has anybody ever told you your laugh sounds sexy over the phone?"

"Wow, no! And thank you!"

"Bob! I don't think I'm paranoid. This car is following me."

"Hold on; my other line is ringing. Hello! Hello! Hello!" There was no response, so I clicked back over. "Bob, can you hear me?" My voice was now a bit shaken.

"Yes, I'm here."

"The call that came in, no one said anything, so I just hung up. Do you think it's the people following me?"

"Erica, I don't believe anyone is following you. I think it's a coincidence that you and the car are going in the same direction."

"What about the phone call?"

"Maybe whoever called didn't have a signal and couldn't hear you."

"Well, I don't see it that way. You may just be right. I'm expecting a call from my boss who is away on vacation. The call could come in any minute now … Perhaps the signal is low. Bob, I might be a little touched in the head to giggle at my own jokes, but I suggest you laugh too when I make them; that's if you want to get on my good side."

"Demanding and feisty, I like it!"

"Hold on; my other line is ringing again … Hello!"

"Hi Erica, this is Dr. Wang. My secretary said you had an emergency."

"Yes, sir. First, I apologize for interrupting your vacation time. I know your time with family is important to you. Okay, straight to the point. I called to give you an update, and I'm nervous about your response. Last weekend, I was brutally attacked. As a result, I have a concussion, broken eye sockets, and some bruises. Sir, I'm in so much pain, and as such, I won't be able to return to work now. I need time to heal, but I'm nervous because I have three big corporate meetings to attend in a few days."

After I was done talking, I gripped the phone tightly, expecting the worst.

"Erica don't worry about the corporate contracts or meetings. Focus on getting better so you can return to work soon."

"Thank you. Thank you, Dr. Wang. I was so scared about my job."

"Erica, you are a big asset to the company. I appreciate all your hard work and effort. Get the short-term leave form from the HR Department. Fill one out and submit it for documentation. Everything will be okay. If you need me, please don't hesitate to call my secretary; she will get in touch with me."

"Thank you, sir. Have fun during the rest of your vacation."

"Thank you too. Good day, Erica."

"Hey Bob, are you there?"

"I'm still holding on."

"Oh, it sounded like you hung up."

"Sorry about that. I had to inform my boss about the incident. I also needed his consent to take a short-term leave."

"Erica, would you like to grab a bite just before you get here?"

"I ate a little something this morning, but I can eat again, though."

"Okay, umm. I'm on my way to Walmart. You could join me there, then we'll go to my house together."

"Okay then. Send me the address of the Walmart."

"Sounds good. I just sent you the location; it's not too far from my place."

"Alright, I'll hit you up when I get there."

"Sure. See you soon, feisty one."

I giggled and hung up.

After I hung up, the mystery caller rang back. However, when I answered, I was greeted with the same silence I'd gotten earlier.

"Hello! Whoever you are, please stop calling my phone. Just so you know, my phone has a call track app, so the police are tracing this call." I could hear the caller's breath, so I added, "So, you're just going to breathe into the phone and not say anything, huh?"

I was still ranting when the car behind me suddenly accelerated, hit me from behind, and swerved off. "What the hell!? Oh my gosh! Oh my gosh!" I immediately dialed 911.

"Hello, 911! Hello, my name is Erica. A black car, I think, has been tailing me, and just ran past mine. It swerved after hitting the back of me, then drove right off."

"Please calm down, ma'am, what is your name?"

"Erica Jackson."

"Erica, everything will be okay. Do you need an ambulance?"

"No, I don't need an ambulance, but I would like a police officer."

"Okay, ma'am. Where exactly are you?"

"I'm at the corner of Boulevard and 96th Place."

"Are you alone in the car, and is anyone else hurt?"

"I'm alone, and no one else is hurt. The other car has left the scene."

"Were you able to see the plate number of the car?"

"No, it happened so fast."

"Okay, the cops are on their way; stay on the line until they arrive. Erica, is your car out of the way from traffic? I want to be sure you're not in any danger."

"Yes, my car is parked on the right side of the shoulder."

"Okay. Don't you worry, the police are on their way. Did you see the driver?"

"No, the car was tinted, but it had a 'do not kick me when I'm down' sign taped to the back window."

"Okay, great. Anything else you can describe about the vehicle? What color was the sign?"

"The sign was in bold white letters. The police are here, thank you, dispatcher."

"This is Officer Brown, and I am Officer Whitaker. May I see your driver's license, insurance, and car registration, please?"

"Here."

The officer collected the documents from me, went back to the car, ran my license and registration, returned to the vehicle, and began, "Wow! It's you."

"What do you mean by 'it's you'?"

"You're that girl from the television, the one that resisted arrest."

"Officer Whitaker, I have no idea what you are talking about. There was no arrest, and that incident has nothing to do with what's going on now."

"It has everything to do with it."

"Okay, sir. Can you just give me my police report so I can be on my way?"

"You can pick up your report at the police station."

"I don't want to go to the police station, sir; I would like my report here, now. There isn't any justifiable reason for me to go to your station."

"Drop the high society attitude before you find yourself behind bars."

"I don't have an attitude, officer. I just want my report so I can be on my way."

"You are yelling and being aggressive with us."

"Officer, how am I aggressive? You know what, just forget it. Can I leave now?"

"No! You'll leave when I say you can leave."

Afraid of what the racist men in blue would do to me, I decided to call Bob to be a listening witness. "Bob, I'm glad you picked up. The two cops 911 sent to me asked for my insurance, license, and registration. I gave them what they requested. However, after they ran my license and registration, they noticed I'm the lady from the television."

"What did they say to you?"

"They started making a fuss, saying I'm being aggressive and that they will lock me up."

"Lock you up for what?"

"I have no idea. I asked to leave, but they said I should sit back in the car. I called you after I got back in."

"Okay. Now calm down. They already put your name in their system, so whenever a cop runs your information, they already know who you are. They are trying to build up a paper trail against you to make it seem like you're always giving the cops problems so that when you sue their asses, they have evidence against your misconduct. You become their number one enemy once you file paperwork against corrupt police officers, city, and state. They will try to scare you off with threats and harassment. Just relax and stay calm when they talk to you. Don't speed off or give them a reason to pull you over after you leave. Alright! I'll be on the phone with you. It's disturbing to see so much hate in the world. It's even worse that someone can see someone else doing something wrong and keep mute."

"The cops are coming to the car window."

Officer Whitaker began, "Please, ma'am, step out of the vehicle."

"Why do I need to step out of the car? I am the victim here. I called you guys, remember?"

"Step out of the vehicle, ma'am."

"Officer, can you please explain why you want me to step outside of my car? I am afraid for my life right now. Can you call your sergeant to come here?"

Bob immediately screamed from the phone, "There's no reason for her to step out of the car. She is the injured party, c'mon. You guys are just bullying her. This is not right."

"Tell whoever is on the phone to stop screaming; we are not listening to him, and we are not bullying anyone. We just want to make sure you are okay."

"You can ask if I'm okay, Officer Whitaker. There's no need for the extra drama."

"Ma'am, the only drama here is you not stepping out of the car. If you don't willingly step out of the vehicle, we will have to drag you out."

"Drag me out for what?"

"Erica, can you hear me? Erica, can you hear me?" Bob asked pensively.

I felt the tension in his voice. "Yes, I can hear you."

"Just step out of the car so you can be on your way," Bob shouted.

"Put the phone down, ma'am, and step out of the car. Put your hands on the hood." Officer Whitaker yelled.

"Why are you trying to search me? It's against the law for a male police officer to search a woman. Can you call a woman to search me instead? And what exactly are you searching me for?"

"We smell weed on you, and you seem high."

"Officer, I don't even smoke. You're making shit up."

"Put your fucking hands on the hood and spread your legs." His tone had turned aggressive.

Tears started rolling down my face as vulnerability and helplessness overwhelmed me. I felt like I was being violated in the middle of the road. Officer Whitaker made me spread my legs. He rubbed his hands up and down my body. His partner just watched and laughed; my humiliation was hilarious to him.

"Nice breasts! You sure are lucky this is a busy road. The things I would do to you."

"Pat her ass down again and make her feel the heat," he jeered as his colleague finished his search.

"Your turn to pat her down," Whitaker said and stepped away.

"Officer Brown, please don't do this." His face was full of dark, lustful expressions. He didn't budge, so I started screaming, "Help, somebody, help me! Please, somebody, help me!"

Some cars slowed down to find out what was going on, but then Whitaker would yell, "Stop resisting!" and they would move on.

As Officer Brown pressed his weight up against my body, I felt the pain in my back from my previous injury even more. He slowly touched my inner thigh till he got to my vagina. Then he squeezed it very hard.

"We know you Black women like it rough! You love it when a man takes it by force. I'll only say this once. If you ever come for any of my partners in my department, we will come for you. We'll hunt your sexy Black ass down and kill you after we take turns fucking you. You hear me, bitch? We will kill you slowly … Get the fuck on." He shoved me from the back, then they both walked back to their squad car.

When I got back in the car, I noticed Bob was still on my cell phone. I was unable to express what had just happened, so I just hung up. While I was still sobbing from frustration, hurt, and disappointment, I prayed to God for strength and guidance. My mind must be playing tricks on me because as the squad car drove off, I could see the phrase "justice for all" boldly written on the back of their vehicle.

I was too nervous about driving, so I called another friend; I wasn't in the mood for Monica's overreaction. Aubrey's long-ass voicemail said, "Hi! You have reached Aubrey, but unfortunately, I am too busy, and you are not that important for me to come to the phone, but if you leave your name and number, maybe I'll call you back today. If not, I'll catch up with you when I'm available. Adios."

Pfff, typical Aubrey. She needed to consider changing her stupid voicemail. I decided to try one more time. As it rang, I inwardly repeated, "Please answer the phone. I need you now more than ever."

She answered, "Hey girl, I was just dialing you back. What's wrong?"

"Aubrey, everything is wrong," I stated in between sobs.

"What's wrong, Erica? I can't understand you. Stop crying so I can make sense of what you're saying. Oh my God! Erica, stop crying. Please stop crying. Where are you? Hold on. I'm calling Monica."

"No, don't call Monica!"

"Hey, Monica! It's me, you, and Erica on a three-way call Erica. She is hysterical and she's crying. I cannot make out what she is saying so I called you to listen. "

What's wrong, E?" Monica asked.

"Somebody fucking hit me from the back as I was driving. So, I called 911, and they sent some cops. When they arrived, they asked for my information, and I gave it to them. Nonetheless, when they ran my name and saw I was the lady from the news, they turned on me."

"Did they hurt you again?"

"What do you mean by 'again'?" Aubrey yelled.

"When you were away on vacation, Erica's house was burgled, she called the police, and when they showed up, they conveniently assumed she was the bugler, tackled her to the ground, giving her a concussion, sprained wrist, and a broken eye socket."

"What the heck? You're pressing charges, right?"

"The cops sexually assaulted me this time. They made me get out of the car and rubbed all over my body. They threatened to gang rape and kill me if I press charges against any of their partners."

"Where are you? We're coming to get you right now!" Monica exclaimed.

"I am at Hot Deluxe Coffee shop, sitting in my car."

"We will be there in 20 minutes."

"See you in a few."

They both hung up.

Erica closed her eyes and thought to herself…. *my eyes.*

These bastards will pay! Every one of these racist animals will suffer. I promise myself that. No one will ever take advantage of me again.

Dry your eyes, put on your thinking cap, and figure some shit out. Find a good plan and how to execute it.

Stop talking to yourself, Erica.

Leave us alone, the voices in my mind said. *What would Aunt Ruthie do?*

Erica, you have to do something. If you stand for this, you will stand for anything.

Yes, I'll do something.

What? Whatcha gonna do?

I don't know yet, but I know they will feel every bit of pain that I'm feeling right now.

See? We agree; revenge is the only way. Make them suffer for all the people they have done this to.

For all the people in the world that have experienced injustice at the hands of police officers, I say no more, no more, no more!

I slammed on the steering wheel as I had this dialogue with myself. People walking into the coffee shop couldn't help but stare. Someone tapped on the window, and I raised my head. It was Monica. She waved. I stepped out of the vehicle to join her and Aubrey.

"Erica, have you lost your damn mind? Aubrey and I watched you as we pulled up. You were talking to yourself and banging on the steering wheel," Monica said. "Aubrey,

Erica will ride with you. I'm going to follow y'all in her car. We are going back to my house."

"Alright, bet!"

The ride took forever. All I wanted right now was to take a nice bath in Monica's huge guest bathroom. I want to wash the filth of those evil men off my body, soothe my muscles, and relieve the pain in my body. I never realized how big and beautiful Monica's house was.

CHAPTER 4
Too Little Too Late

"Good morning, sleeping beauty!"

I stirred awake. Monica was staring at me with a mixed expression of worry and joy.

"That guy, Bob, called you all night until 3:00 a.m."

"Oh shit. Thanks, Monica. I was supposed to link up with him yesterday, but with all that drama, I truly forgot."

"Erica, what's up with you and this guy? He seems to have appeared out of nowhere."

"Be nice, Monica. He offered to help me. He asked me to stay at his house after someone broke into mine."

"Erica! Seriously! Nobody knows this man. You can't be serious about staying in this dude's house when we don't know who he is, where he comes from, or anything about him, for that matter."

"Where is Aubrey?"

"Don't change the subject."

"No, seriously, where is Aubrey?"

"She left last night. After you fell asleep in the tub and almost drowned, if I might add, we laid you down in the guest bed. We figured you needed rest. She left afterward. I, on the other hand, went to sleep. Are you going to tell me about this Bob guy? Can we at least meet him so we can put our minds at ease? I don't trust anyone with everything going on, especially this knight in shining armor. There is something about him that doesn't sit well with my spirit, and I haven't even met him yet."

"You are skeptical about everyone."

"Yes, I am. And you should be too. When you trust people too quickly, before truly getting to know them, bad things happen. It always happens like a wake-up call. And usually, by the time you're awake, it'll be a little too late. You're my best friend. I admire, respect, and love you, and I want nothing but the best for you. To see you in so much pain and hurt bothers me."

"Monica don't start crying; you're going to make me tear up, and honestly, I've cried enough these last few weeks. I have no more tears to cry."

"How about you stay here with us, at least until we figure out who broke into your home?"

"To be honest, I don't want to impose on your family."

"Come off it. You're family and family sticks together. I'm not taking no for an answer. C'mon! It'll be like the good old days when we were kids, sleeping at each other houses, telling scary stories in the dark, and sneaking snacks upstairs in bed."

I smiled. "Yeah, those were the good old days. Life was easier back then."

"Life is what you make it."

"True indeed, Monica!"

"What's on your agenda today?"

"I want to talk with the out-of-state lawyers so I can start suing the police department, city, and state."

"Where did you find those lawyers?"

"Well, Bob found them for me."

"Bob?! See, he's doing too much already."

"Stop it, girl. He's fine."

"Nope! Until I meet him, he's the crazy man."

I burst into laughter. "He's not crazy. You're making me laugh my ass off. You're the crazy one. I mean, you used to stalk your husband before y'all met, remember, Monica?"

"Yeah, I agree. And crazy recognizes crazy," she said, laughing as well. "Are you hungry? I can fix us some hotcakes, eggs, sausage, bacon, cheese grits, toast, and fresh-squeezed orange juice."

"You already know the answer to that. My mouth can taste the food right now even as you speak, and my stomach is in my back due to hunger pains. Get the food popping, and please, please, whatever you do, do not burn the toast."

"FYI, I do not burn toast. It's called Cajun style."

"Well, cook my toast American style; we're not Acadian people."

"Breakfast will be ready in 30 minutes. Make your calls, then come downstairs."

"Yes, Mommy dearest!"

I dialed Bob immediately after she stepped out.

"Bob. I'm glad you picked up. I was preparing to leave a voicemail if you didn't answer. First, I want to apologize about last night; things really got out of hand. My two best friends came and picked me up after the incident yesterday. I ended up falling asleep at Monica's house. Just so you know, Monica and Aubrey are the names of my best friends. I decided to stay here for a while; they're like the only family I have."

"It's okay. But my offer still stands. Whenever or if ever you decide to come to stay at my home, you are always welcome."

"Thank you! I'm about to contact those lawyers. I'll keep you updated. Catch up with you later. Enjoy your day!"

"You, too!"

Next, I dialed one of the lawyers.

"Good morning, thanks for calling Weaver and Berman Civil Rights Attorney at Law. This is Melissa speaking; how may I address your call?"

"Thank you, Melissa. My name is Erica Jackson. I would like a free consultation to discuss my case with a lawyer."

"Okay, great! Before we get started, I'll need to get some of your personal information, if you don't mind. May I have your address, email address, and telephone number, so I'm able to call or locate you just in case we get disconnected from the phone?" "Sure, the address is 509 W. Phillip Ave, 30303, Atlanta, Georgia."

"Is this a house or an apartment?

"It's a house. My email is EricaJackson@tasoul.org."

"In the next few minutes, I will email you an Incident Complaint Form. In your words, describe exactly who, what, where, why, and how the event happened. Include hospitals, doctors, nurses, and witnesses if applicable. Be very descriptive. List any short- or long-term injuries. Your response to this outline will be sent directly to an attorney. The attorney will contact you within 24-48 business hours. Is there anything else I can do for you, Erica?"

"No."

"Alright. Thank you for calling Weaver and Berman, Civil Rights Attorney at Law; have a safe and great day."

"You, too!"

Once I was done with the call, I noticed the aroma of Monica's cooking. I rushed downstairs.

"Monica, the food looks good. And no burned toast either."

"Yeah, whatever. Sit your bougie ass down and eat your food while it's still warm."

"The only thing missing is fresh-cut flowers in the center of the table."

"I keep telling your monkey ass that you're bougie as hell. So, I was supposed to cook the food, then go into the garden and cut flowers just for you, huh?"

"*Sí!*" I answered in Spanish.

"If you want flowers, go get them yourself. And this house is a Spanish-free zone; we only speak the English language up in here."

"*La proxima vez que venga, tengo mis malditas flores en la mesa,*" I called in Spanish.

Monica's face rumpled as I rattled off the syllables. "What the hell did you say?"

"I said the breakfast was terrific," I responded, laughing my ass off.

"Habitual liar; that's what you are."

"What are we doing for the day?" I asked as I wiped the tears that had formed in my eyes from the laughter.

"Let's go shopping, E."

"Monica, that's obviously a bad idea. Shopping doesn't work when both of us are involved. We end up arguing every time. And the problem is always the same: Monica wants to see all the shoe stores, but she wants to buy nothing. It's either the price or it's the shoe. Whatever it is, we just end up going to all the shops only to come right back where we started, with Monica trying on the exact shoe she started with. Just this explanation alone is giving me a damn headache. No, thank you. Call Aubrey; y'all can shop together."

"Nah, Aubrey's shopping taste is too rich for my blood. In the stores she shops in, a pair of shoes cost the same as my mortgage. I'm not spending $2500 on designer shoes. I live on paychecks, while the people I give my money to live from one house to another. Nope! It's not in my DNA to be stupid. I believe in savings and investments, not spending till I'm broke. That's the problem with the people of today; they would rather give their last dollar to the rich who travel on yachts and sip expensive wine. Take the money you spend on expensive shit that holds no value and invest in your community. Open your own shoe store or clothing line. Shit, do something that will create generational wealth."

"Monica, you said that as well as if I had articulated that message. Glad to know you listen and take notes when I speak."

"You're being irritating, Erica," Monica groaned.

"Why are you trying to sound like me when you have never talked about building wealth before? You know that's a controversial subject I debate about."

"No, I'm not trying to sound like you. You think that if anyone has an opinion on a topic that sounds remotely close to yours, that person must envy you. But you don't always practice what you preach, Erica."

"What the hell is that supposed to mean?"

"You are always talking about what Black people should do for the community, but what have you done for the community?"

"Are you shitting me right now? With my hard-earned money, I bought a run-down apartment building, fixed it up, and rented out units at reasonable prices so they're affordable for low-income families. None of my units are section 8. Section 8 prices ensure the father, or the man of the house is never around because he is too busy working whatever number of jobs to make sure he pays the rent and provides for his family. By and by, he is deprived of the opportunity to contribute to raising his children and play his part in their growth and development physically, mentally, and otherwise."

Erika continued. "High prices for apartments are one strategy our government uses to dismantle the Black community; the plan is to break down the family structure of the Black community. This problem is what inspired my Oasis project. I discovered the problem and I'm working tirelessly to bring a lasting solution. My building Oasis helps low-income families and families with credit problems attain affordable housing. My team and I host credit repair workshops and parenting training classes. How dare you question me, Monica?"

"Okay. Since you like to ask questions, let me ask you one. What exactly have you achieved, Monica? You married into wealth, so you didn't earn any of it. And the disturbing part is, if Anthony, your philandering husband, were to leave you today or tomorrow, you would be sleeping with the homeless people in a shelter because you have no money of your own. You gave up your career for a man, and he made you sign a prenuptial agreement. Don't you ever attack my character or integrity!"

"Of course, your career is all you ever worry about. You have no family, no man, and no children. You have nothing but late nights and wet sheets with random men," Monica said in retort.

"Really, Monica? That's how you see me? And you say all this because I expressed my opinion? You're funny. Well, don't come running to me when Anthony decides to leave your ass for another woman again."

"Get the hell out of my house!" Monica finally yelled.

"With pleasure!" I snapped back.

"Don't you dare slam my door either!" she screamed.

I grabbed my keys and stepped out of her front door, leaving it ajar.

As I drove off, I called Aubrey.

"Greetings and salutations," she said.

"Hey, AUBREY!" I yelled.

"Do you always have to be so damn loud on the phone? Dang!"

"I see you're snappy today; you probably didn't eat your bowl of kibbles and bits."

"Yeah, I got your kibbles and bits. What do you want, E?"

"I was going to ask you to ride with me to the party store; I want to buy a few things for my birthday dinner party that's scheduled to happen in two weeks, but with your low vibrational energy, I'm not sure I still want you in my space."

"Hold up. Why did you wait until the last minute to plan a dinner party?"

"It's been on my mind for a while now, but with so much going on, I forgot. Are you going or not? You are holding up my progress!"

"Yup. Count me in."

"Good. I just pulled up to your house. You have 10 minutes. I'm waiting."

"Hahaha. Ten minutes is not enough time to wash my ass."

"Take a birdbath like you do when you're in restaurant bathrooms."

"FYI, I am slutty on those nights. Today, I want to be a lady."

"Hopefully, soon, you'll decide to stay a lady."

"Erica, are you throwing shade right now?"

"Yes. Now hurry, I am hungry."

"Would you like to have some of my kibbles and bits?"

"Less talking and more washing, Aubrey."

"Okay."

"Use soap this time."

"The things that come out of that mouth of yours, Erica, make me want to puke."

"No, no, no, Aubrey, it's not that at all. It's all the vanilla cream sitting at the bottom of your stomach; you're regurgitating babies."

"Disgusting, ugh!" She then hung up.

I knew that comment would get her ass off the phone. Once she hung up, I started playing *Real Love*, my favorite song by Mary J Blige. The sound of music was blasting from my car when suddenly someone banged on my window.

"Excuse me. Excuse me, miss!"

I paused the music and let down the window.

"Hi. My name is David, and I'm Aubrey's neighbor. This is a quiet block. Your car music is so loud I can't even hear my television. Can you please turn it down?"

"Mr. David, that's your name, right? Well, unfortunately, I don't like your approach. You were banging on my glass window just to get my attention, but there was another way you could have done that. And who exactly are you to tell me how loud my music can be? It's not even that loud."

"It is. And it's disturbing the neighbors."

"That's a bald-faced lie. I don't see anybody else, just you here complaining."

"But I've asked you nicely to turn the music down."

"Pink chicken, man. If you don't get your ass away from my car—"

"If you don't turn it down right now, I will be forced to call the police."

"Sir, you can call the army if you like. I truly don't give a damn."

Aubrey sees the exchange, leaves her house, and runs toward my car. "Hold up, hold up! What is going on here?"

"Your unfriendly and aggressive neighbor banged on my car window and told me I can't play my music on this street, and he will call the police on me if I keep at it."

"David, go back inside. I'll handle this."

David walks away. He gives me an angry look as he does.

"E, it's time to roll out; let's go."

"See? This is the problem with people. They're always trying to mind someone else's business. I was chilling, singing, and enjoying my sister's song when that troublemaker came along and started banging on my damn window for nothing. Stupid prick!"

"Erica, you're focused on the wrong stuff. Tell me about the dinner party you're planning and why you walked out on Monica."

I roll my eyes. "I see Monica called you already. Monica and I had a disagreement. But she started the whole thing. As for the dinner party, it will be at my house. It's a small, intimate, semi-casual dinner party with a maximum of 30 guests. And of course, it'll be catered."

"Will you send Monica an invitation?"

"I'm not sure yet; she said some pretty awful things to me."

"Both of y'all always say mean things to each other when y'all mad. True friends should never cross the line; you should never be disrespectful to each other."

"To be honest, Aubrey, I feel on the inside Monica has soft hate towards me."

"Why do you feel that way?"

"Every time we get into an argument, she doesn't hesitate to bring up my man-less status. When it's not that, it's about me being career driven. She is either attacking me for not having a man, or she's attacking me for being career driven. I think she silently hates that I'm career driven. Maybe it's because she gave hers up for a man who gives her everything she could ever want or ask for but is emotionally disconnected and cheats on her from time to time."

"Worse still, she's always striving to portray them as some power couple, even though deep down, she is miserable. I want her to be honest with herself; stop putting on airs and false illusions to fit into society's standards of what a relationship should be. Too many people are walking around pretending to be happy, in love, and sexually satisfied. She clowns me for not being in a relationship and owning up to my single status. I'd rather be by myself than be with a man that lies, manipulates, cheats, and mistreats me. If that's the kind of man she wants, oh well, that's her choice. Yes. I have accepted her and her choices; that's what it means to be a good friend. She shouldn't belittle me for wanting better; it's my choice, and she should make peace with it like I have made my peace with hers."

"Okay, okay," was all Aubrey said.

I changed the subject. "What are you wearing to my dinner party? Don't wear anything too revealing, so you don't offend the other women. You already know men; they'll stare or follow you around all night long even though they came with another woman. That right there is an anecdote for drama, and I want a drama-free event."

Sarcastically, Aubrey responded, "I'm wearing sweatpants and a t-shirt from Something Light Clothing Line."

I just stared at her.

"Don't worry about what I'm wearing; just know it'll be perfect for the occasion. But seriously, I do need a favor from you. My friend Will is an up-and-coming fashion designer, and he could really use some marketing tips from an expert. Could you help him out for me? His website is www.somethinglightclothing.com."

"Okay, okay, I'll look," I said. "But again, mind what you're wearing, and don't get too crazy."

Aubrey made a silly grin and began, "What's going to happen if I do? Your female friends are insecure with their bodies, and philandering husbands aren't a reason to dampen my styling and profiling. The Almighty God created my body shape, and what He gave me is a blessing. You and your friends should get you some and stop focusing on me."

"Aubrey, you are taking it the wrong way. We're both blessed to have hourglass figures. But the thing is, these days, not all women are completely right in the head, and you don't want to attract the wrong type of attention or catch a case with a jealous woman. I'm just looking out for your safety. The women of today are not playing when it comes to their men. Some may run you over with a car because of jealousy. Some resort to shooting, stabbing, and even murder. Once they perceive you as a potential threat to their family, they come for you full throttle. If you don't believe me, go on social media; you'll see videos."

"Again, insecure women are not my problem or my fight. Now, what's next?"

"I guess nothing since you don't want to listen."

"Chill. I could care less about what other people's issues are."

"Well, on that note, I have nothing more to say on the subject."

Finally, she got into my car, and we were off to the mall. Returning with loads of bags, I popped the trunk.

Aubrey stopped in her tracks, scanning for a space to fit the bags she was carrying.

"Why do you have so much stuff in your car? What are you making with acid, batteries, PVC pipes, double-sided tape, and wire? Your trunk is so full; there's nowhere to put your bags."

"I'm working on a project at home," Erica answered. "Be careful, don't hurt yourself with all these supplies."

"One may think you're trying to blow up something. It looks serious. Is this project a secret? You haven't mentioned it before."

"No, it's not a secret. Hush, Aubrey! Just put the bags in the car, please. And what's with all these questions? I've done so many projects before, and you've never shown interest, so don't start being intrigued now. Meanwhile, what time are you coming to help me decorate and prepare the food for the dinner party?"

"Yeah, yeah, fine. Continue your secret project. And just remind me the week of the party."

"Aubrey, store it in the calendar on your phone and set a reminder. I have so much going on, I might not remember to call you."

"Damn, E! Why are you being such a bitch? I got shit going on, too. You're not the only one with a life. I don't want to forget, and you snap at me like you're snapping at everyone else."

"This is the thing with you people. I'm not snapping or attacking anyone. When you ask me for a favor, I make sure it goes on my priority list. I hate making promises and not following through. I've been everyone's counselor, therapist, friend, sister, mother, helper, etc., but whenever I need any of you guys, I have to hunt y'all down. Can't y'all be there for me like I am there for y'all? Is that too much to ask?"

"Are you okay, Erica? At the rate you're attacking people, I'll be shocked if anyone shows up for your party. Ever since the police hurt you, you've been distant, mean, and coldhearted, even towards your friends. We love you, and if you need to express what you feel inside, we are here."

"What exactly can you do for me? Can you hide the bruises on my face? Maybe you can stop the world from seeing me as just another Black woman and treat me as a human being. You have no idea what I deal with every day: racism, sexism, and social injustice. You'll never know the conviction of being a Black woman because you come from an interracial background, and you pass yourself off as a White woman. When you fill out forms, you don't check off Black or African American. You check off Caucasian."

Erika continued, "The way society treats you is different from the way it treats me, and that's unfair. I live in fear of being harmed because of the color of my skin. I have nightmares because of what those racist bastards did to me. Well, they will pay. I promise you; they will pay."

Aubrey sighed. "I think you should talk to someone; you may have PTSD."

"Yeah. Yeah, I guess. Well, I'm sticking to Hammurabi's code: an eye for an eye, and a tooth for a tooth. It has all the answers I need. And stop psychoanalyzing me. You're pissing me off."

Aubrey's expression turned to fear and worry. "Erica, you're scaring me. What is the Hammurabi code?"

"Where were you during history class in school? Probably didn't go to school that day," I replied with a dark smile.

CHAPTER 5
Maybe, Maybe Not

Officer Whitaker was finishing up paperwork at the precinct, impatiently looking at his watch now and then. His shift was almost over, and he was anxious to be free so he could let loose. He was off all weekend and looking forward to relaxing. His partner, Officer Brown, looked over at him, shook his head, and laughed.

"Hey man, you look like a crack fiend counting down the time to his next fix!"

Officer Whitaker chuckled. "I guess you could say that. Megan's coming over later tonight—I just can't get enough of that sweet ass of hers!"

"Oh, that's why," Officer Brown replied, rolling his eyes. "Get a grip man; I know this isn't your first time getting some ass. Just don't let her see you acting crazy like this or else she'll own your soul and your balls. These women can smell a simp from a mile away."

"Simp? Hmph, not this guy. She knows exactly where I stand. There's plenty of fish in the sea; she's just the catch of the day!"

"The day? Try the month—or rather, the last couple of months. You've been seeing this chick exclusively for a little while now. It may be too late for you, man. You're almost at the border of Simp Town."

Just as Officer Whitaker was about to respond, he received a text. "Great, she's leaving work now and gonna get ready to come over. That gives me enough time to go to the bar and have a few drinks."

"Dude, how are you going to the bar if she's on the way to your place?"

Still looking at his phone, Officer Whitaker mindlessly responded, "She can let herself in, she has the ke—" He realized what he was saying and stopped short, but it was too late. His confession was out, and his partner just stood there, staring at him in disbelief.

"No fucking way. You gave her a *KEY TO YOUR HOUSE*?!"

"Dammit, you weren't supposed to know that. Look, I'm fine with her having my key. She tidies up around the house and does my laundry. Sometimes, I'll even come home to a meal she cooked and left in the microwave for me. Who's doing any of that for your lonely ass?!" he shot back.

His partner continued looking at him as if he didn't recognize him. "I was wrong. You're not at the border of Simp Town—you're the fucking mayor!" He laughed hysterically.

"Yeah, whatever man," Whitaker said. "The mayor is still the boss, and she knows that's exactly what I am. And I'll have plenty of instructions for her tonight; so, on that note, I'm out of here. I'll catch you on Monday!"

"Hopefully, you'll still have testicles by then!" Brown yelled after him as he was making his way out the door with his middle finger up in the air.

Two hours later, Whitaker had his fill at the bar and was ready to go home. He was tipsy but not full-blown inebriated. Megan had texted him about 30 minutes earlier and said she was already there and would be waiting. He entered the home, staggering up the stairs. He heard the shower running.

He fell on his bed and shouted into the bathroom, "Hey babe, you ready for this big cock?"

A silhouette came out of the bathroom, wet, naked, and ready said, "I'm ready to take every single inch of you, baby."

As he lay back, she climbed on top, straddling him. She grabbed his shaft so hard, he said, "Oh wow, you want it rough tonight, huh?"

"Yes, I'm in that kind of mood."

"Well, how rough do you want it?"

"So rough that you'll be dead asleep by the time I'm done with you."

"Well, goddamn!" he said excitedly. "You sound kind of crazy, but I like it!"

"Oh, we'll see," she replied.

As she slowly bent over to kiss him, she suddenly jolted up and jammed a needle into his thigh.

"What the fuck!" he cried out in utter shock, but that's all he could say as the lights turned on. Once his eyes adjusted to the light, he realized it wasn't Megan he was talking to. But he couldn't get up because whatever he was stuck with made him unable to move.

"You ... you're that Black bitch I pulled over a couple of weeks ago!"

"Yeah, and I'm about to show you who the bitch is. Now you're going to squeal like the filthy, fucking, pig you are!" She reached under the bed and grabbed the machete she had hidden there.

As the officer lay there paralyzed and helpless, he pleaded with the intruder. "No, please don't do this. You know what will happen if you kill me? The entire police department will turn this whole fucking city upside down looking for you. You don't want that, because if they find you, you'll wish you—AHHHHHHHH!"

A blood-curdling scream escaped his lips before he could finish as he watched the intruder slice his manhood clean off and hold it up for him to see as she laughed victoriously, blood running down her hand and wrist.

"AHHHHHHH! YOU FUCKING BITCH! I'M GONNA FUCKING KILL YOU!"

"I guess they will need the entire police force to find little ol' you!" she quipped as she paused to look pathetically at his castrated manhood. She then raised the machete over her head.

"NO, PLEASE!" Whitaker cried, to no avail.

With all the force the intruder could gather, she chopped off his other head.

*****

As guests trickled in for my party, they were in awe of the beautiful décor. The color scheme of black, gold, and burgundy made my already regal-looking home even more distinguished and lavish. Everyone loved it, but they weren't at all surprised; I knew how to throw a party! The live band played all the party hits: "Before I Let Go," "Electric Slide," and "Don't Stop 'til You Get Enough." The open bar and catered food were top-notch as well. I spared no expense for myself and my guests.

"Girl, you really outdid yourself!" my colleague Cynthia said. "I need to keep this band and caterer in mind for my future events!"

"Nothing but the best for this boss chick!" I proudly responded. "Make sure you try the fried calamari—it is so damn good!"

As I continued to work the room and mingle with the guests, I soaked up all the accolades and well-wishes. I loved being the center of attention, and tonight was my night—nothing could ruin it.

The music faded. *Ting, ting, ting.* The sound alerted the guests to shift their attention to the large foyer. Monica stood up, holding a glass of champagne. As she began to speak, the guests were served their own glasses of champagne.

"Good evening, everyone! This is a packed house tonight, and I'm so glad we could all come out to celebrate Erica's birthday with her. I just wanted to take a moment to tell you all what a wonderful friend she's been to me. I'm truly inspired by her drive and ambition, and I believe she's an example to us all of the kind of life we should endeavor to live."

At that moment, the doorbell rang. A server went to the door and saw a package left on the ground outside, but no one was there. It was a white package with a pink and yellow ribbon around it. I walked over and decided to open it. Obviously, whoever left it wanted to show off their gift, and I was more than willing to oblige.

A note was situated on top of black tissue paper. It read: "Cheers to those who wish me well, and all who don't can go to hell." My smile quickly turned into a frown. Wrapped in the tissue paper was an old black barbie doll with a rope around its neck. Gasps could be heard from the crowd, then murmurs.

I tried to calm the guests down, but just as I started speaking again, a news broadcast interrupted me and stopping the smooth jazz music playing from the television. The face of Officer Whitaker, the cop who had assaulted me, was displayed on the screen.

"Turn up the volume!" someone said. The news anchor informed the audience of the murder of Officer Whitaker.

Bob turned and said, "Hey, that's one of the cops who beat Erica up at her home."

The news anchor continued to explain that the officer's girlfriend was found beaten, unconscious, and tied up in his basement closet. Everyone looked at me as I abruptly left the room.

As I was making my way upstairs to my master bathroom, I felt an uninviting chill overcome me. I went to the sink to rinse my face and quell the nausea of what I was experiencing. As I put my head up, I thought, *What was that riddle about?! Who was it from?* As I stared deeply at my reflection, I saw a dark figure emerge from the shadows behind me. I turned quickly, but no one was there. I let out a sigh of relief and scolded myself. "Get it together, Erica."

I went back downstairs and announced that the party was over. A clearly intoxicated Aubrey stopped me and said, "You okay, girl? You can tell me if you did it," she whispered.

"Maybe, maybe not," I sharply responded, and brushed past her to continue herding my guests out the door.

CHAPTER 6
Family Secret

After the last guests left, I locked the door and dimmed the lights in the house. I was perplexed. My celebration had not gone as planned due to the news of the sudden death of the officer. Although I was relieved that he would never be able to do to anyone what he did to me ever again, there was this unsettling feeling deep inside me; something was not right about the circumstances of the murder. But for now, I desperately needed to relax, so I ran a bath, lit candles around the room, and poured a glass of my most expensive Cabernet Sauvignon. I took several sips, and as the plethora of sweet, soothing aromas from the candles filled the air, I sank into the tub and went into a deep, meditative state. As I reached over for my glass to take another sip, a dark cloth was slapped over my face to blind me. Before I could scream, I felt the pinch of a needle in my neck. And then, nothing.

I emerged from my unconscious state feeling groggy and weak. I tried to sit up and realized I couldn't, as both my hands and feet were tied to the bed. As my eyes adjusted, I realized I was in my cabin in the mountains of Hooperville County. "What is going on? Am I having a nightmare?" I wondered aloud. Across the room, a girl was playing with Barbie dolls. She was facing the corner, her back to me. As I squinted to get a better look, I realized the figure's stature was that of a grown woman.

"Who the fuck are you? Why are you in my house?!" I demanded but did not get an answer.

The woman was too busy to notice I was speaking, as she was deep in conversation with her dolls.

"Hey, Daddy, where are my mom and sister?" one doll said.

"Mom took your sister to a family member's house," replied the other.

"Why, Daddy?"

"Because your mom is *FUCKING CRAZY!*" the woman screamed.

I was officially over playtime. "Look, bitch, I ain't got time for your commentary! Who the fuck are you?" I yelled.

"You're gonna have all the time in the world by the time I'm done with you," the woman calmly said.

Slowly, she turned to meet me face-to-face. I was speechless, in a state of shock and fear, as my own face stared back at me.

"Cheers to those who wish me well and all who don't can go to hell. So, you don't wish your sister well? Or would you like to go to hell?" the woman asked.

I immediately remembered the riddle that was delivered to my front door at my birthday party. I fell deeper into a state of confusion. *Who is this woman? How does she know about the package?*

"Sister? I don't have a sister. What are you talking about?"

The woman glared at me with deep hatred. She stood up and shouted, "Why do you think your mother is in the fucking nuthouse now? Selling her offspring for a profit, without a thought!" My eyes grew wider as she continued, "Yeah, that's right, you weren't born alone. All this time, you didn't even know you have a twin sister. Well, allow me to introduce myself, sis! My name is Eva."

I could not believe what I was hearing. My heart was beating so fast it could have popped out of my chest. I looked at every inch of Eva's face and body, seeing features that were identical to mine.

"I understand. It's a lot to process," Eva continued as she walked closer to me. "So, let me give you a break from your crazy and successful life; you deserve and need it!"

With that, she lunged at me and stabbed my thigh with a large needle, and almost instantly I was out once again.

*****

Eva exited the cabin and jumped into Erica's Mercedes Benz. Filled with diabolical glee, she turned on "Get Out the Way" by Ludacris and blasted it through the speakers. She stepped on the gas and zoomed through the mountains as she made her way to Lennox Mall. She spent four racks at the mall, going from store to store, fulfilling her heart's every whim. As Eva was heading to the food court, she ran into Aubrey.

"Hey Erica!" Aubrey called who she thought was her close friend. "It's good to see that you're doing better because you didn't seem like yourself at the party the other night. I want to apologize for my drunk ass and the smart-ass remark I made about your involvement with that police officer's death. That was totally inappropriate of me and that wasn't the time and place for it, so I'm sorry."

Eva internally had a moment of slight panic. *Who is this chick? Does she know? This is obviously one of Erica's friends.* "Girl don't worry about it. That cop got what he deserved, anyway," Eva responded.

"But on another note, look at all these bags! Looks like somebody was tearing through here and didn't bother to let their shopping buddy know so I could come along for the excursion!" Aubrey said, sounding disappointed.

This bitch is annoying, Eva thought. *I need to ditch her, quick!*

"Are you still going to Anthony's grand opening?" Aubrey asked.

"Yes," Eva stated curtly. "Not to cut this short, but I have some unfinished business to take care of. See you soon!" She rushed off.

In Aubrey's mind, this was an odd interaction. Usually, Erica greeted her with a hug or a sarcastic remark. But whatever business she needed to attend to must have been really pressing, so Aubrey just let it go.

Eva power walked through the parking lot and eventually made it to her car. Once inside, she breathed a sigh of relief. "I better get acquainted with her associates," she said. "They just better stay out my way or else they can catch hell too!" She turned the ignition on and pulled out of the parking lot.

Once home, she opened the bottle of Crown Royal she had bought from the liquor store. *This bitch is bougie as hell with all this weird-tasting wine,* she thought.

As she took a sip of her drink, the doorbell rang. "Yasssssss!" she exclaimed. "My new furniture is here so I can get rid of this she-she poo-poo decor." She hurried to open the door, only to be met by Monica and Anthony standing outside.

"Hey girl!" Monica said. "We just stopped by to check how you're doing."

Eva didn't know who this woman was, nor did she hear a word she was saying because all she could focus on was this fine specimen of a man standing next to Monica. *Got damn,* she thought, *he could definitely get it!"*

"Earth to Erica!" Monica said loudly.

Eva snapped back to reality. "Oh, hey, come in."

"'Oh, hey?' Is that all you can say to your best friend?" Monica asked. "I guess this is what our friendship has come down to."

"Ain't nobody even thinking about you, girl. I'm waiting for my new, fly-ass furniture to get here," Eva responded with a stank face.

Anthony chimed in. "Well, we just wanted to see how you were doing. We know you've been through a lot lately, but we want you to know we care about you and we're here for you. Now, if you ladies will excuse me, I'm going to use the restroom."

Hold up, I'm tryna come too. In every way possible, Eva thought as she eyed the print in Anthony's sweatpants as he walked away.

"So, what have you been up to? I know we haven't talked much lately, but what's new? You have any plans tonight?" Monica asked.

"I have a date."

"Really? With?"

"Don't worry about it, *chica*; it's not your concern!"

Monica was perplexed. "Erica, why are you not telling me what's going on with you? We're supposed to be best friends and I don't even know who you're dating. This is crazy!" In her mind, however, she thought the mystery guy was probably Bob, which made her even more agitated.

"Crazy that I'm going on a date? What kind of woman would do such a thing? Yeah, that's realllllly crazy!" Eva said sarcastically.

"You know what I mean, Erica. But it's fine. Enjoy your date. I hope it goes well," Monica said as she walked away towards the powder room.

"That's all you had to say the first time," Eva said. She then made her way upstairs to grab the invoice for her furniture order to make sure the delivery was accurate once it arrived. But she also wanted to get a moment alone with Anthony.

Just as she reached the top of the stairs, he was exiting the bathroom. As he was walking by, she reached over and slapped his ass.

Anthony was startled. "Yo, what are you doing?" he strongly inquired.

"I just wanted to see if your ass is as hard as everything else on you," she said with a sly smile.

"Erica, I don't know what's up with you, but this ain't cool. My wife is downstairs, you trippin'!"

"Oh, just relax. I'm only playing around with you, bro. Loosen up, it's all good fun. Don't go running to tell Mommy," she said, referring to Monica.

Anthony said nothing. As he made his way downstairs, the doorbell rang. Monica was just exiting the powder room, so she opened the door and let the delivery guys in. After saying goodbye to Eva, the two left.

LYNELL SMITH

CHAPTER 7
Eye for an Eye

Over the next few weeks, Eva continued to live it up, enjoying Erica's lavish lifestyle: attending parties, making expensive purchases with her money, and making it rain at Onyx, where she used to dance and hang out with her cronies from her old neighborhood. As she was throwing cash around, she saw two familiar faces in the club—one near the dance floor and one in VIP. She smiled to herself and said, "This is gonna be a very eventful night."

She would recognize that body structure anywhere, and those lips … mmm, yes, it was him! The dancer who had his attention was really working it. 'Lollipop' knew her stuff, and patrons paid very well to be entertained by her. Anthony was no different—Eva could see her movements had mesmerized him. But Eva already had in her mind she could (and would) have him caught up with her.

Then, her attention was averted to another recognizable face. Officer Brown, the partner of the late Officer Whitaker, was also in the club. Eva began salivating. With deviant glee, she thought, *Oh, I'm about to get my shit off in more ways than one!* Already tick-tocking in her head, she called over Big Petey the bouncer.

"Wassup, doll face. What you need?" he asked.

Eva licked her lips. "You know you can help me in a lot of different ways," she responded as she looked him up and down. "But for tonight, I got two stacks for you. Tell Lollipop to take that gentleman over in VIP to a private room and keep him entertained for 30 minutes. Have a stack waiting for her when she's done."

"Okay, babe, you know I got you," Big Petey said.

Eva then grabbed Big Petey's smooth, thick beard, and pulled him close to her face. Petey was at full attention—in every way.

"Then, you see ol' boy over there?" she pointed at Brown. "I need you and Jerry to escort him to the alley where the locked gates are with no cameras. Make sure the music is blasting, 'cause you know what I'm about to do."

"You need help with that, babe?" he eagerly asked, ready for some action.

"No, I got it. All I need is that machete."

"Okay, well just let us know when you are ready for the clean-up."

"Of course. Thanks, Petey."

Eva went to the locker room and grabbed the machete she used on Whitaker from her old locker and then made her way to the alley.

Back inside the club, Anthony asked Lollipop, "Why am I being taken in here? I didn't pay for a private dance."

"Oh, it was already taken care of for you, love," she replied.

See, they doing too much, Anthony thought, referring to his friends. But Anthony didn't mind the sight. After all, it was more than what he was getting back at home. So, he sat back, relaxed, and enjoyed his private time with Lollipop.

Outside the club, Mobb Deep's "Quiet Storm" blared through the speakers. Eva was practicing her axe-throwing skills as Officer Brown was tied up to the gate 15 feet from where she was standing. He was already missing his right hand—a testament to how good Eva was at this game. As blood trickled down his elevated arm and soaked his outfit, Eva stood there laughing.

"So, how do you like being sacrificed for mere pleasure?"

As screams of agony muffled by the blasting music escaped his lips, Officer Brown grappled with the understanding that these were his final moments, and no one would ever see him again. As promised, Big Petey came outside to clean up the mess. Eva handed him his cash and then went back inside the club and walked into the private room where Lollipop was holding it down for her. She gave her a kiss on the lips and slid 10 Franklins into her bosom. Anthony looked up, horrified.

"*OH, SHIT!* Erica, what are you doing here?! Please don't tell my wife!"

Lollipop exited the room with a smirk on her face. Eva told her to lock the door and turn on the red lights, indicating the four-camera view was on inside the room.

"Yo, what's going on, Erica?!" Anthony shouted.

Eva pulled down her pants, revealing her panty-less posterior. As she was bent over twerking, Anthony became weaker.

"This is what's going on," Erica replied. "Now, stop being a punk, and come get this."

Anthony's heart was racing as he vacillated about the choice in front of him. This was his wife's best friend. To call this foul would be a severe understatement. But he was already here, and in his mind, Erica was trustworthy and would keep the secret. *We're grown, we'll just keep this between us*. He then unbuttoned his pants and grabbed Eva, easing his way in.

*****

Eva's alarm clock awakened her. She stretched in bed as she looked at the mirrored ceiling she had installed in Erica's bedroom and said, "Damn, what a night." Anyone else with half a conscience would have condemned such sinister deeds, but the combination of sex and murder aroused such an exhilarating rush within her that she needed a release before starting her day. As she was approaching climax, the doorbell rang.

"Oh, GO AWAY!" she exclaimed as she continued pleasing herself, intent on not stopping until the job was finished. The doorbell rang four more times before it was over. Eva then rushed downstairs to see who was so pressed to visit her at 8:00 a.m. With her robe partially open, revealing one of her nipples and a portion of her nether region, she opened the door to two detectives, who both seemed slightly irritated at having to wait outside for so long.

"This better be really important for you to be blowing up my doorbell this early on a Saturday morning," she angrily proclaimed.

"Ma'am, do you mind tightening your robe, please?" one detective asked.

Eva looked down at her robe, and with unbridled sarcasm, she stated, "Oh, this? Sure. You gentlemen don't seem like you're into women, anyway." She obliged their request.

The detective ignored her and introduced himself. "My name is Detective Brunson, and this is Detective Stevens. We're here to discuss Officer Jarrett Brown, who was brutally murdered last night. Do you know anything about that?"

"What are you asking me for?" Eva responded.

"Security footage pulled from Onyx shows you were there last night," Brunson stated matter-of-factly. "So, do you mind if we come in to ask you a few questions?"

"Yes, I do mind," Eva objected. "I have shit to do today."

"Ma'am, we're going to ask you to come down to the precinct for questioning," Stevens said. "We're identifying individuals who were present at the establishment last night, and since you are one of them, we need to rule you out as a suspect."

"Fine," Eva said with exasperation. "I'll come down, but not without my lawyer present."

"I'm not sure why that's necessary, especially since you're not considered a person of interest, but sure, if that's what you'd like. You have that right."

"Great. See you in a couple of hours," Eva said, before rudely slamming the door in the detectives' faces. She then immediately called her lawyer. "Hey, I'm gonna need you to meet me down at the 37th precinct. They want to question me about that officer that got murked at Onyx last night."

"Okay, I'll be there," her lawyer responded.

*****

I woke up again in my cabin, wondering how long I'd been trapped down there. From what I could gather based on sunrise and sunset, I hadn't eaten in two days. Frantically, I kept looking around to determine what I could use to help free my hands, but I could not find anything.

I was in shock I had been kidnapped and even more shocked I had a twin sister that I knew nothing about. I tried to piece MY childhood memories together to determine if I'd ever received any clues about Eva's existence. There had to have been some inkling of a secret my mother was keeping. Despite the constant pondering, I could not come up with anything. *How could Mom give one away and keep the other?*

*****

At the precinct, Eva was led to the interrogation room where her attorney was waiting for her, along with the detectives.

"Alright gentlemen, I have engagements tonight, so let's make this quick!" she demanded, determined to make the process difficult for the detectives. If she had to have her time wasted, then they would also regret their decision to summon her there. For starters, a simple answer to any of their questions was, well, out of the question. She tormented the officers with her sarcastic answers regarding her knowledge (or lack thereof) of the murder.

"Ms. Jackson, at one point on the night of the murder, you left the club and then returned about 90 minutes later. Where did you go?" Brunson inquired.

"Where did *you* go the night of the murder? Some brotherhood you all have. One of your own got mangled and you couldn't even save him. If I was a cop, I wouldn't trust any other cop, even if my life depended on it. And if I was that officer, I'd be in the afterlife putting hella hexes on the entire police force right now!"

"Ms. Jackson, please just answer the question."

"Seriously, though. You oughta be ashamed of yourselves. If you can't even save your own, then what's the point of protecting the community at-large?"

Detective Brunson was visibly frustrated. Between Eva's smart mouth and the valid points she was making about his colleague's untimely demise, this was going nowhere.

"We'll be in touch. We'll get your cooperation one way or another," Brunson promised.

Eva's attorney rushed her out of the district speedily. "Congrats, you just made more enemies. They suspect you now."

Eva turned to her lawyer. "I don't give a fuck about what they believe. Let them bring it; no one has ever met the real me."

The attorney appeared dazed. He changed the subject. "Just be careful. There are more of them than you."

Eva got out of the car, which had just pulled up to her house. She got out, walked over to the driver's side, bent over, and dipped her head inside. "They better be more scared of what I might do. Once you cross me, you will always be an enemy forever."

The lack of fear in her eyes made her attorney's mind run wild.

*****

Eva got in her car and drove off, saying, "Let me go get a ham and cheese sandwich for this Barbie doll and lace her with some more sleeping potion." As she stopped at Sammie's to pick up Erica's food, she noticed a gorgeous, tall Latino with broad shoulders and piercing light brown eyes. His sun-kissed skin glistened as his uniform shirt choked his bulging biceps.

As Eva was heading into the establishment, he was heading out. The two locked eyes and nodded at each other as they passed by. Eva had no choice but to look back while still walking. And to her surprise, the officer was looking back at her too! Again, they locked eyes, but this time, they both stopped in their tracks. The officer motioned for her to come over. Eva, not one to take orders from any man, obliged and seductively floated over to him. There, in the middle of the parking lot, they talked.

"How you doin' today, beautiful?" he inquired.

"I'm doing great, especially after getting some attention from you," Eva responded.

Her honesty made him let out a hearty chuckle. "And rightfully so, because I couldn't help myself. My name is Victor," he said as he extended his hand.

Eva softly grabbed it and gave a light shake. "Erica. Nice to meet you."

"The pleasure is most definitely all mine," Victor responded while looking her up and down. "Here, take my number, and call me sometime."

Eva pulled out her phone and typed in the digits he recited. She then texted him to secure her number in his phone. "I'll be hitting you up soon," she said.

"Well, soon can't get here fast enough," replied Victor with a broad smile. "In the meantime, you have a wonderful day."

"You, too!" Eva said as she started to walk away but decided to give a quick glance backwards. Her eyes became fixated on his tight chest and the bulge in his pants. She then refocused, picked up the sandwich, and headed to her sister's cabin.

*****

When Eva arrived at the cabin, she came downstairs to the basement to find me awake and screaming at the top of my lungs.

"You prissy bougie bitch! No one can hear you, so stop the damn noise before I hush you up!"

"LET ME GO!" I screamed at her more.

"Oh, nah, lil' baby, I can't do that."

"Then what the hell do you want from me?!"

Eva stared at me as if I was ignorant and could not understand her circumstances. So, she made it plain by detailing how she was raised in a dysfunctional home with an alcoholic foster mother and perverted stepfather who molested her day in and day out once she became a teenager.

"Do you now see where I'm going with this?" Eva asked, looking intently at me.

I looked back at her, still dumbfounded.

Ready to snap, Eva went over to the shelf by the utility sink and grabbed a face mirror. She then brought it over to me and shoved it in my face. "We share the same face, sis! I want and will have your life; everything you took for granted will become mine: your money, your car, clothes, and yes, your friends. By the time I'm done with you, you'll wish you were dead." Eva stood up and began walking toward the stairs.

"By the way, your friend Monica has a handsome husband; I can't wait to taste that. I see how he looks at you, Erica—oh, I mean me, Eva," she said with a deviant grin.

"Eva, you don't have to do this. Please, I beg you, don't do this!"

"Aht-aht, princess bougie Erica. Do not beg, that's not a good look on you. You just sit tight while I work my magic. Goodnight!"

Despite my screams, Eva poured water into my mouth to quench my thirst, duct taped it back up, and made sure I was securely tied up. Then she turned off the light and left.

CHAPTER 8
The Body Collector

⁓

Eva and Martinez met at The Compound, which was Eva's idea because she didn't want to give the impression she wanted anything more from him than a short, good time. After checking her coat, she walked over to the bar. Martinez was already there, cocktails prepared, and waiting for her.

"Oh, look at you, just ready and waiting to get me liquored up," Eva said, taking the drink from his hand and smiling slyly.

"It's called a Laffy Taffy," Martinez replied as he looked at her seductively. "Something tart with a tinge of sweetness."

"Who says there's anything sweet about me?" Eva asked.

"Only one way to find out."

Eyes deadlocked on each other, they both devoured their drinks in a millisecond and exited the club. Martinez took Eva's hand and escorted her to his SUV, which was parked on a secluded side street. They had barely closed the doors before ripping each other's clothes off. Not one to be submissive or allow a man to take the lead, Eva climbed on top of Martinez. She could feel his thick, bulging manhood throbbing through his jeans.

Martinez went in for a kiss, but instead was met with a hard, perky nipple shoved in his mouth. Surprised, but still down to do it her way—the nasty way—Martinez licked, sucked, and nibbled until Eva felt satisfied with that breast and then shifted him to the other. Meanwhile, she had unzipped his pants and taken control of his manhood, massaging and getting it nice and prepped for her. Then, without warning, she pulled her miniskirt above her waist to reveal her panty-less, well-groomed lady-part and slowly slid down onto Martinez's thickness. All he could do was grab a hold of Eva's tight ass as she rode on top of him, working him as he let out moans of absolute pleasure. Eva wasn't satisfied with that, though. She wanted his soul.

"Tell me you like it," she whispered in his ear without breaking rhythm, licking, and nibbling his earlobe in the process. She then reached down, wiped some of that wetness off his shaft with her finger, and then put it in his mouth to taste.

Martinez was somewhere else. Just for a moment, he took his eyes off Eva's curvaceous body bouncing up and down on him to say, "You know, I don't usually go for mature women like yourself, but goddamn, this is so good!"

"Oh, you usually like to be in control, huh, Officer? Well, sorry, I'm not that type. Now shut up and lick this kitty." Eva reclined the seat all the way back and sat on his face. Muffled moans were all she could hear as she felt Martinez's tongue work her labia. The sensation of him sucking and nibbling like his favorite piece of candy had her trembling as he squeezed her cheeks. Eva's vision blurred as she faced the back window, reaching her boiling point.

Martinez knew how to work his tongue; Eva couldn't remember the last time she had gotten head this good. Finally, she couldn't hold it in anymore. She let out a moan so loud it left her wondering if it could be heard despite the windows being up. Not one to be outdone, she got off Martinez and folded down his second-row seats. Martinez watched as he wiped his mouth of Eva's nectar. Once the seats were folded and there was plenty of space in the back, Eva got in the face down-ass up position, and in the sexiest voice said, "Come finish me off, baby."

Martinez pulled his pants down to his ankles and positioned himself behind Eva, but not before taking a nice bite of her ass. He then slid inside, starting with slow strokes as he gripped her waist. It was Eva's turn to moan as the strokes picked up the tempo. Martinez stayed on rhythm, smacking Eva's ass every so often. As he stroked, Eva stroked back.

"Yeah, that's right baby, stroke me back," he commanded. "*DAMN*, you're being such a bad girl!"

"Oh, I'm a real bad girl, baby," Eva responded. "Teach me a lesson, Officer!"

"Oh, I'm about to," Martinez's voice trembled as his back shots got faster and harder.

Now Eva wanted him to have total control, but she knew it was she who was really in charge.

"Release on my back, baby," she said as she innocently looked back at him. Judging from the look in Martinez's eyes, she knew it: mission accomplished. Martinez's entire body was visibly shaking at this point. His breathing was heavy, and he looked as if he was about to cry as the sweat dripped from his forehead.

*****

Eva pulled up to AJ Construction, ready to show up and show out. Even though she had the thrill of her life with Martinez a few nights ago, she couldn't stop thinking about her romp with Anthony. In fact, since their encounter at the club, Eva had been stalking him at his business, doing pop-ups, and making sure all eyes were on her.

As she entered the building and made her way up to Anthony's office, she saw a young woman exiting. Her long brown hair and caramel skin were a dead giveaway of her Latino roots, possibly Puerto Rican. The two were laughing and seemed extremely chummy together. Eva immediately smelled sex in the air. Not literally, but she sensed the vibe that there was more between them than just coffee and paperwork.

The young woman breezed past Eva, saying, "Good afternoon," with a slight head nod.

"I'm sure it is," Eva sarcastically replied with a scowl. Without hesitation, Eva made her way into Anthony's office. "Um, who was that?" she demanded without even a proper hello to Anthony.

"First, hello to you, too. Second, that's my new secretary, Melissa Hernandez. I've been training her all week."

"I bet you have," Eva retorted, not letting up on her sarcasm.

"What's that supposed to mean? Never mind, it doesn't even matter," Anthony said.

"Nope, it sure doesn't," Eva agreed, "because I know your wife would have way more of an issue with you frolicking with me than that wannabe J. Lo."

"What are you talking about, Erica?" a bewildered Anthony asked.

"Nothing baby, it's our little secret, right? No one has to know … as long as the price is right."

"Oh, so now you want to be a whore for hire? Or you're blackmailing me?"

"Call me what you want, but I've got the goods and you know it. I also have a big mouth," Eva stated, looking at him intently.

You definitely ain't lying about that, Anthony thought. looking at Eva's curvaceous figure all the way up to her mouth. He couldn't help but think of his last encounter with her, and how her mouth had worked wonders. Anthony wanted to keep her quiet, at least until they could have fun a few more times, which would also give him time to figure out how to deal with this situation moving forward. He concluded that whatever she was asking for was a small price to pay to not blow up his life.

After the talk with Anthony, Eva decided to follow the pretty, green-eyed Melissa out of the parking lot. Not knowing where Melissa was headed, Eva patiently followed along until she was well outside the city limits. Melissa pulled up to a beat-down trailer home in a trailer park community. When the car pulled into the driveway, a little boy ran out of the house and hugged Melissa.

Oh, great, a little boy. I know you have no choice now, Eva mumbled in an undertone. She then rushed over from her car and called out to Melissa. Melissa looked perplexed because she realized this was the lady who had made a scene at her workplace.

"Who are you and why are you at my home?" Melissa asked.

"No need for formal introductions. Just know I'm your nightmare," Eva said as the little boy looked up at her.

"Go in the house, Rico," Melissa commanded her little brother. Waiting until he was safely inside, Melissa then continued, "Now what do you want?"

"Looking at your living conditions, you could use some money. So, I'm propositioning you with this offer: I'll give you $30,000 cash if you will quit your job and leave

Anthony alone. I know you're screwing him, but most importantly, you will help me sabotage his company's new city contract."

"What?! No, I can't do that," Melissa replied, in shock at such a brazen proposal.

"You can and you will, or that precious little boy will mysteriously disappear for good."

"Are you threatening me?!"

"Honey, I don't do threats. I see you haven't been watching the news. People are going missing every day, and body parts are being found. Don't fuck with me. You do as I say and when I say it and we will all live in peace, or you can decide not to do what I say and live your life in misery. I told you, I'm your nightmare."

Melissa was dumbfounded and afraid of the audacity of this woman to show up at her home and make such crazy demands. But that was just the thing. Eva's actions signaled she meant every word and would not take no for an answer— regarding anything. Melissa looked back at her brother as he stared out the window. She knew she had no choice. With tears rolling down her face, she looked at Eva and nodded. "Okay."

"Perfect!" Eva responded with a perky smile as if Melissa was a willing participant. She then stepped closer and gave Melissa clear instructions.

CHAPTER 9
Lust of the Frenemy

onica's husband Anthony was hosting a new grand opening of his construction building. Eva was intent on being both the talk and life of the party. She pulled up to the building in her Mercedes and stepped out wearing a sexy, red, fitted off-shoulder dress with a slit that ran up to the edge of her upper thigh. The dress was sure to make every man's eyes pop out of his head.

Eva approached Monica and Anthony to congratulate him on his endeavor. With her hips seductively switching, she slowly walked over and hugged Monica, saying, "Hey, girl." She then hugged and kissed Anthony on the cheek, leaving her red lipstick print on his face and the smell of her perfume on his tuxedo.

Monica snarled but kept her composure in front of the other guests. Monica grabbed her arm and pulled her to the side. "What are you doing? I told you the other night on the phone that I was wearing red and no one else should be in red."

"Monica, I forgot, and you know red is my favorite color."

"I don't care, Erica! This is my man's night and you're ruining it."

"Oh girl, stop being so dramatic! The night is not ruined; come on and let's drink up all this cheap ass wine." Eva walked away and started seductively dancing in the middle of the floor while everyone stared at her in disbelief. Aubrey, who saw the exchange between the two from across the room, walked over to Monica.

"Monica," Aubrey whispered in an undertone, "what is wrong with Erica? She's acting different. I saw her the other night driving from King's World Restaurant when I beeped the horn at her she gave me a lame-ass wave and kept driving."

"Yeah, something's definitely off with her," Monica agreed. "I think she just made a pass at Anthony, too."

"What?! Oh, hell no, let's confront her together."

"Not here!" Monica sharply responded. "This is Anthony's event; we'll handle this another day."

"Okay, your choice, Monica, but if she made a pass at my man, all drinks would be flying in the air."

"Aubrey, stop! You're trying to get me hyped."

"No need to get hyped—you need to whoop ass!"

Meanwhile, on the dance floor, Eva was moving her hips in slow motion to the music, caressing her body from her hips to her breasts. This was a black-tie affair, but Eva's sensual dancing was making it borderline X-rated. All eyes were on her, and she reveled in every minute. She danced her way to Monica and Aubrey; their stank faces were fixated on her.

"Why are y'all two heifers staring at me like I'm your frenemy?"

"Erica, are you okay?" Aubrey asked.

"Yes, just a little toasty, that's all. Why do you ask?"

"Because we're worried about you—you're acting funny, making a pass at Monica's husband, and coming here with this red dress on. You're being really arrogant and not so friendly."

"Well, kiss my not-so-friendly big ass!" Eva stated in a loud voice that caused some heads to turn.

Anthony rushed over to the ladies to intervene in the quarrel. "Ladies, please, this is not appropriate. This is my night, so whatever issues you're having can be dealt with another day. Erica, please, you're being a bit disrespectful."

"Oh, I can show you disrespectful, Mr. Anthony!" Eva looked him dead in the eyes, and he knew exactly what she was talking about.

"Look, just relax." Anthony stared back at her before storming off to the bar.

Monica followed him, vehemently apologizing. Aubrey looked at Eva and shook her head before walking away.

After things simmered down and the festivities continued, Eva went to the bar and ordered a Hennessy and Coke. Anthony was still there, sipping his Old Fashioned. Eva asked him to come to the house to fix her kitchen drainpipe because the water was draining too slowly. Anthony looked at her in disbelief.

"You know that shit you pulled wasn't cool, right? Being on your grown and sexy tip. Yeah, we did something together, but what's done is done, so just chill, Ma."

Beyond toasty at this point, Eva looked over at Anthony and said, "Just shut the fuck up and let me enjoy my drink. I'm not thinking about none of y'all right now."

Anthony shook his head and walked away.

Monica approached him. "What did she just say to you?" she asked.

"Nothing. You're being real aggressive right now at my event, so chill out or I'll see you at home."

"Anthony! Anthony!" Monica called to no avail. He left her standing there to speak with his guests.

*****

A few weeks later, Eva was in the kitchen cooking breakfast when she saw the news flash across the screen. Officer Martinez had been found dead. It was so sad, because she'd really liked the guy. Staring at the screen, she got lost in space, thinking about that day.

She'd broken into his home to surprise him one day by being naked in the kitchen when he got home—the perfect snack. But instead, he'd already been at home, and she'd found him molesting his daughter in the living room. Eva couldn't believe her eyes. She was filled with rage. She was also conflicted because if she were to intervene in the act, then her identity would be exposed, so she had to leave the child there. But she vowed to make sure that child would never hurt again the way she did.

The following evening, Martinez's daughter went over a friend's house, and he invited Eva over for some Netflix and chill. He had the nerve to motion her over to the same couch he had molested his daughter on the day before. Eva obliged, cozying up to him. And just as Martinez thought she was reaching up her skirt to pull off her panties, her hand quickly reemerged, brandishing a knife. She had slit his throat, castrated him, then set his body on fire.

She knew the police would not suspect her, because Martinez, who was married, had had extramarital affairs on the job, and he had a good rapport with several prostitutes. Eventually, any leads the police had went dead. Little evidence was found due to the smoke and fire damage at the home. However, the entire community was now on alert that a cop killer was on the loose, armed, and extremely dangerous. The FBI had been called in to assist with the investigations of the murders. The city was hot, but it made no difference to Eva. She reveled in the drama.

A few days after the party, Anthony reached out to Eva to schedule a time to look at the kitchen drainpipe. They decided that 3:00 p.m. was the best time for both of them. When Anthony arrived at Erica's home, R. Kelly's "Bump and Grind" was playing so loud it could be heard from outside on the front step. Anthony rang the bell but got no answer. He rang it again with the same result. He then turned the knob, and the door opened.

"Hello!" he called as he walked in. When there was no response, he yelled louder, *"HELLO!"*

"I'll be right down! You can go in the kitchen," Eva yelled back. "I'll be right down."

Anthony turned on the sink and laid inside the cabinet underneath the sink to investigate the issue. Eva came downstairs and stopped at the doorway, seeing this six-foot-four man with a milk chocolate body like actor Michael White. His voice was smooth like Barry White and he walked like Obama. He could have broken the entire sink at that moment and it wouldn't have mattered. Eva slowly started walking toward him and as he was getting up, he noticed her lavender and pink nightgown, which just barely covered her butt.

"Woah! Are you going to cover up?"

"Cover up for what? You are in my house, plus I am your sister, remember?"

"Erica, please, can you put something on? I am still a man."

"Yes, you say you're a man, but I haven't seen manly yet."

They both chuckled, and he laid back under the sink.

"Erica, can you hand me the wrench?"

"Sure." Eva stood over him as she handed him the wrench. As he looked up, he saw she was not wearing any panties. "Erica, please don't do this to me."

"Do what? I'm just handing you the wrench like you asked," she said while bending down to him with her legs wide open for him to see. "I see you staring—do you like what you see?" She slowly took his hand and rubbed it up her thighs into her moist inner lips. "Yeah, I see you like it." She forced his fingers in and out to the beat of the song.

Unable to hold back anymore, he jumped up and gripped Eva by the ass and laid her on the wooden dining room table. She slowly unbuckled his pants and slid her hand down to meet his hard wooden stick. Both hearts were beating so fast until Eva asked the forbidden question, "What about your wife?" He got up and apologized for allowing the situation to get this far.

Eva then grabbed his face as he turned away in shame, and passionately kissed him so hard that he leaned backwards and almost fell. He kissed her back, and it was there on the table where Erica hosted her dinner parties and people put their food, that they had sex.

"Anthony, Anthony, yes, yes," Eva heavily breathed as he thrust in and out forcefully and ardently.

The two couldn't stop, and the sex was so good Anthony did not see the hidden camera on the fireplace. Now that the shared moment was over, Eva decided to go in for the kill.

"So, when are you leaving your wife?"

"What? I am not leaving my wife," Anthony stated matter-of-factly. "What has gotten into you, Erica? All these years, you never came on to me before, so why now?

"I always liked you, but I thought you were more into Monica. Actually, when we all first met, I was feeling you, but you pushed me off to Monica and I just went with it. Now we can be together the way you wanted to years ago."

"Erica, I have kids with her now—we are a family."

"Well, we can have kids and I can be your family, too."

"Erica, you are coming off as a little deranged." Anthony stopped, took a deep breath, closed his eyes, and composed himself. Once he reached composure, he opened his eyes and stared at her with the utmost intent and resolve. "Read my lips," he calmly stated, "I am not leaving my wife for you or anybody else."

"I'll tell her we slept together," Eva retorted.

"Tell her what you want; she'll take me back—I cheated on her before. Plus, she will never believe you."

"She will once I show her the video of us fucking! Now, how do you want her to receive it—at her parents' home or at your anniversary party?" It was bright and sunny in the room, but Eva's evil smirk made the atmosphere dark and dreary.

"You bitch! You planned this the whole time?!"

"No, you did once you went balls deep in me at the club that night. It was a good fuck though, so don't be mad."

After Anthony left, Eva went to the small cabin and told Erica about her escapades with Monica's husband. Erica didn't believe her, so she popped the DVD containing their deviant sexual act into the player next to the TV. For the next few minutes, Erica helplessly watched as the outward reflection of her physical features violated the sanctity of her relationship with her best friend. Tears rolled down her eyes as she whispered, "Oh God, Monica."

"He was pretty good too; so now I see why Monica won't leave. But soon he'll become my husband," Eva declared with the same evil grin she had flashed at Anthony.

As the days went on, Eva harassed Anthony and Monica by calling in the middle of the night, visiting their home unannounced, and picking up their young child from school to get ice cream. Nervous about her behavior, Monica told Aubrey what was going on. Aubrey decided she was going to confront the person she thought was Erica at her house. When she pulled up, she heard people arguing inside. Curious, she hid in the bushes, attempting to be as incognito as possible since it was broad daylight outside.

"Tell her what you want; she'll take me back—I cheated on her before. Plus, she will never believe you."

"She will once I show her the video of us fucking! Now, how do you want her to receive it—at her parent's home or at your anniversary party?"

"You bitch! You planned this the whole time?!"

"No, you did once you went balls deep in me at the club that night. It was a good fuck though, so don't be mad."

Aubrey was speechless yet infuriated. "You're supposed to be Monica's best friend, you slimy ass bitch!" she said underneath her breath through clenched teeth. She was definitely going to deal with Erica.

Once Anthony left, Aubrey acted as if she was just arriving at the house. Anthony barely said hi and brushed past her, exiting in a hurry. Unable to hold her composure, Aubrey stood in the foyer with the front door open and told Eva what she had heard. The two got into a heated discussion, and Eva knew she had no other choice. She invited Aubrey into the house and locked the door.

Two days later, fishermen found a car at the bottom of the river, but there was no body. The car was registered to Aubrey Miller.

CHAPTER 10
Happy Anniversary

"So, if you'd like, we can go with the airy, pastel theme or do something a bit more regal using colors like gold and burgundy or purple with cream accents."

Monica stared at the color cards laid out on her coffee table. She was trying her hardest to be present with her event planner, but she just couldn't shake the overwhelming void she felt not having her two best friends with her to help plan her 20th-anniversary party. She hadn't eaten in 48 hours, as she was worried sick about Aubrey and hoped the police would find her.

"Um, I—I think we'll do—"

Her ringing phone cut Monica's train of thought. She rushed over to the kitchen counter to answer it, hoping someone was on the other end who had information about Aubrey's whereabouts.

"Hello! Hello! Yes, this is she … okay … yes, I can do that—when? Okay, sure, I'll be there shortly. Thank you, goodbye." She then went back into the den to let her event planner know they would have to continue meeting another day, as she had an urgent matter to attend to. As requested over the phone, she made her way to the police station to speak with detectives about Aubrey's disappearance.

Once at the district, Monica met the detective she had spoken to on the phone. He asked questions about the last time Monica had spoken with Aubrey and if she may have expressed concerns or had any conflicts prior to her disappearance. Just as Monica was about to respond with a resounding no, she remembered the verbal exchange between Erica and Aubrey at Erica's birthday party.

Reluctantly, Monica told the detective about Erica's suspicious behavior lately, but the detective just dismissed it as women quarreling over a man. Monica didn't think so and continued to press the issue. While detailing the last time she saw Erica, she suddenly felt dizzy. She tried to ignore the feeling and focus, but the room just spun faster and faster until she could not articulate her words. And then she blacked out.

"Mrs. Johnson … Mrs. Johnson!" the detective called to no avail. He immediately called an ambulance, and Monica was rushed to the local hospital.

*****

Anthony paced endlessly within a short margin of the hospital's desk counter, waiting for a response. The reel of impatience seemed unending. He'd arrived at the hospital shortly after he'd received news of his wife's loss of consciousness. A host of thoughts had since popped in and out of his mind, all negative, while he waited on the nurse for a response.

"She is in room 306, sir," the nurse said.

Anthony thanked the nurse, but the sight of Eva halted him. Her presence stilled his raging worries yet registered a fresh set of more torturous ones. She walked past him like he wasn't there, greeted the nurse, and continued toward Monica's room. It would seem she'd already obtained Monica's room number, having arrived a little before Anthony.

"What do you want this time, crazy bitch?" Anthony started, dragging her to a corner by a corridor that led to the elevators, granting them somewhat makeshift privacy. He attempted to block off Eva from any movement. He was keen on an explanation.

Eva chuckled, shaking her head in open disappointment. She was living her best life, and what foolish Anthony thought didn't really matter.

"Well, since you asked, I came to see my best friend," Eva stated sharply. "But why all the name-calling, darling?" she continued, caressing her hands down his chest, slowly easing out of his grip.

Eva, having mesmerized Anthony out of the way, broke into a quick pace, chuckling ludicrously. Anthony quickly followed behind, hustling to catch up with Eva, who was intently walking fast.

"I don't want you anywhere near my family. If I didn't before, I'm making it clear now; stay away!" Anthony spoke, struggling to keep up with Eva's pace.

Eva was forced to a halt. She turned to respond but was caught off guard by the doors of the elevator steadily sliding open. They both entered, maintaining decorum.

Eva kept tapping her feet anxiously up the three-story ride, eager to unleash the boiling contempt brewing within. *Homeboy is sadly mistaken if he feels he can talk to me the way he just did. My silence isn't to be mistaken for weakness; I just don't have beef with him. But he better watch it.*

"Look here, Mister. Listen and listen well, 'cause I'm not gonna repeat myself. Monica is my friend. Get that into your thick skull. If Monica is in the hospital, then I'm coming over to see her. Sort your shit out yourself. If you want some more good lovin', I can bend over right here," she said, laughing irritatingly. Her serious face back on, she continued, "But what I won't do is allow you to pile shit on me. Ever! I'm not your bougie-ass wife, which means I'm not your doormat. You can't push me around, so be warned!" Eva concluded, pushing past him, and continuing towards Monica's room, which was now two doors ahead.

For a moment, Anthony stood like a wounded lion, just staring into nothingness. The hospital wasn't a place to cause a scene, although he was ready to let loose. But owing to the little maturity he could account for, he decided otherwise.

This crazy bitch is intently trying to ruin my life. But nah! That won't happen. Her plans won't work, Anthony thought.

Still standing where Eva had left him some seconds ago, he watched as his biggest mistake walked into his wife's room. Knocked back to consciousness, he immediately picked up his pace, entering with Eva. His long legs were a proven advantage.

"You're three months pregnant, ma'am. Your blood pressure is high, and we need to get it down to avoid any complications. Until then, you'll be on bed rest."

Anthony immediately turned toward Eva. They stared at each other as though trying to unravel a mystery.

"Wow. Congratulations, Monica. So, I'm going to be a godmother! The Big Guy upstairs is sure doing wonders," Eva finished.

Monica, who had been engulfed with the doctor's explanation, hadn't noticed when the duo walked in. She extended her arms, an invitation for a hug. Eva obliged.

Holding Eva in a hug, she gave Anthony a questioning look. Her facial expression was solid, "Why is this crazy person here?"

Anthony flipped both palms of his hands open in midair in response. The doctor had already greeted Anthony and left.

"Oh, shoot! I have to be on my way, Sis. I got some things to attend to. Catch you later. Bye!" Eva finished, hurriedly leaving the room.

Anthony breathed a heavy sigh of relief. It'd become clear "Erica" was indeed crazy. And how they hadn't noticed for so long was a mystery.

Monica tapped him on the back, jerking him back to reality. She stared at him without saying a word, worry boldly adorning her facial features. "Something is off with Erica. She's been acting a bit strange."

"A bit? Hell no! That lady is outright crazy!" Anthony interjected. "I mean, how did we not see it all these years?"

Monica eyed him but didn't bother confronting his bluntness. She wondered what made him so resolute about his conclusion. Whatever the case, Erica was still her best friend. And Monica was not one to dig deeper and be assertive. She had never even confronted Anthony about anything, not even his cheating habits.

"I'm worried, babe. In all my years of knowing Erica, I've never seen this version of her. We need to do something. I feel I have to," Monica continued.

"Let's not worry about all that now. Just rest up as the doctor ordered. We can deal with Erica and all her madness later," Anthony said, kissing her on the forehead.

*****

The ringing of the doorbell eventually got Marjorie, Monica's mother, on her feet and in motion. She opened the door to find a delivery man with a boxed package that read,

To my darling husband, I love you so much, and I can't wait to see your face when you see this.

Marjorie blushed and smiled. The gesture brought back fond memories that she greatly cherished. She was proposed to similarly by her husband, Monica's father. A small package had arrived at her front door one day when he came to see her. It had been her engagement ring.

Beep, beep. The microwave timer abruptly ended her reminiscence.

"Monica, baby, your package is here."

Monica was too into her thoughts to even acknowledge her mother's words. She'd been searching for her wedding band for a while now but couldn't find it. For some odd reason, it wasn't in her jewelry box. Although she'd heard her mother's call, the compulsion to quickly look elsewhere hadn't allowed for any response. There wasn't a second call, so she continued her search. Frustrated, she gave up.

Emerging from the bedroom after sliding into her finely tailored chiffon gown, Monica was still drawn to check places she hadn't checked. Eventually, she conceded to not finding it, at least for the moment. With beams of vehicle headlights taking turns flashing across her window, Monica knew it was time to head downstairs.

The party was in high gear. Marjorie had helped plan it, and she'd done a great job. After she was remanded to bedrest, Monica knew she would need assistance with planning the anniversary celebration. As the doctor had explained, she needed to keep her blood pressure down to avoid the risk of preeclampsia. Thankfully, she'd started improving after just a few days. She and Anthony had discussed it and agreed her mom could plan the whole thing. It would not be as elaborate as she wanted, but something was better than nothing.

Now, downstairs and seeing the entire set-up, Monica couldn't be happier. She quickly scanned the room for Anthony. Once in sight, she motioned towards him as quickly as she could in her body-fitted gown.

Clink, clink, clink. Anthony tapped his champagne glass with a fork.

"Ladies and gentlemen, a toast to my lovely wife." Anthony paused, looking into Monica's eyes, holding her by her waist, and smiling convincingly. He turned towards his audience and continued. "First, I would like to thank everyone here. You've all taken time out of your busy schedules to celebrate us. And for that, I say a very big thank you. And to my wife, Monica," he turned to face her. "For 20 years, we've had our ups and downs. But through it all, you've stood by me. Even when I didn't like myself, you were there for me. You've given me two beautiful children and now a new joy bug is on the way; well, I hope it's a he."

Anthony paused for effect as his audience laughed at his joke and accompanying facial expression. He then continued.

"I couldn't imagine my life without you. You are everything a man could ask for and more. I was blessed the day I found you. No one has given me the love, time, and affection you continue to give me. You have made these years with you my best years. I will always love you."

With his conclusion, his audience smiled and raised their glasses to commence clinking and drinking.

"Hold up, everyone. Before we start clinking our glasses and drinking our wines, I, too, have something to say," Monica interjected, catching her breath, and bowing her head as if she was trying to get a hold of words. A few stares with wide eyes, up, down and around the crowd, she began speaking

"Anthony, my darling husband. My rock and shield. My prince charming. My knight in shining armor. We've faced many challenges, but we overcame them all because God was and still is looking over our marriage. No one or thing can come between the love I have for you. I couldn't have asked for a better husband. You are a provider, loving husband, and present father to our children. I'm elated to be your number-one cheerleader, friend, lover, and wife. May we continue with many more happy years. Cheers!"

"Woah, woah, woah. Everyone, hold up just a minute. I also have a speech," Marjorie quickly said, causing endearing laughter amongst the guests.

"To my son-in-law, Anthony, and my daughter, Monica, I am so happy to see you guys hang in there. Watching y'all grow together as a couple, building businesses, and changing the community has been amazing. No doubt, y'all are a power couple. May God continue to bless y'all and keep your marriage safe from harm. Cheers! One more thing," she winked at Monica, turned the audience's attention to the television, and continued with the reading of the note, "To my darling husband, I love you so much, and I can't wait to see your face when you see this."

Monica looked confused. She did not have any surprises planned for Anthony, especially since time had gotten away from her as a result of her medical condition. Anthony looked at her face and instantly knew something bad was about to happen. He quickly went for the remote, but not before the damage had been done. In full HD, everyone saw him having sex with Erica—well, Eva, on her wooden kitchen table. Their groans and moans permeated loudly through the surround sound system. He turned towards a dazed Monica, stricken and full of guilt.

"Baby, I can explain."

He tried to hold her hand, but she reclined back.

"Baby, please, I can explain."

Tears were now flowing down Monica's face. To say she was embarrassed was the least of it. She was distraught. Stunned to silence. Just moments after an open exchange of love between each other, now this. With that, as well as other thoughts swirling in her mind, Monica grabbed her keys from the welcome bowl and ran outside toward her car.

"Baby! Wait!" Anthony screamed, following behind her.

CHAPTER 11
Two Faces

———

er foot firmly on the accelerator, Monica sped with intent. Pregnant or not, Erica was about to feel her wrath. Monica started crying again. The scene kept replaying in her mind, causing her tears to intensify. The shame was just too much.

"How could you? Of all the people you could sleep with, Erica? Anthony?! Don't you have any shame?!" Monica soliloquized, hitting the accelerator repeatedly, angrily.

She then slammed on the brakes, causing a screeching sound. She flung the driver's door open and headed towards Erica's front porch. Crouched down to avoid being seen through the windows, she heard voices inside Erica's house. Monica went around the side to get a better view from the window she knew would be open. Erica was arguing with a man.

"Bob, calm down already," Erica said dismissively.

"Don't tell me to calm down. You hired me to do a job, and I delivered. Now it's time to pay up, and you're giving me excuses?"

That name Bob rang a bell. Monica tried hard to remember where she'd heard the name before, then it clicked. It was *BOB*, the guy Erica had talked so much about after her incident with the police. Monica hadn't seen Bob, so she couldn't be exactly sure it was him. But then again, it was Erica's house, and Erica was having a conversation with a guy named Bob. It had to be him.

"First, it was the incident in the gym with Erica. I made that happen. Then you asked for the other thing, the one with the racist officers. I set that up, too. That wasn't even part of the deal, but I came through. Why is it now so difficult for you to pay up? Huh?!"

Monica listened, confused. *Why is Bob talking to Erica like she's not there? What is going on? And what thing with the racist police officers is he talking about?*

Regardless of the confusing dialogue, Monica continued to listen. Whatever was going on, she was ready to find out. Suddenly, amid those prevailing thoughts,

Erica's movements caught her attention. While Bob complained, Erica had poured out some wine and was now putting something in it. It looked like a white pill. Monica covered her mouth with both hands in exclamation.

Her friend then smiled charmingly and walked towards Bob seductively. She had the two glasses in her hands. The one in her right hand had been roofied.

"Oh, Bob. You're always complaining about this and about that. Stop overthinking this! Calm down and have a drink. I didn't say I wouldn't pay. I'm working on something big. You'll definitely get your money. Here," she offered him the glass in her left hand, "have a drink with me. We can discuss payment later."

Reluctantly, Bob obliged, but motioned his hands for the glass on the right instead. "Okay. But I want the other glass," Bob commented, giving her the side-eye.

Eva handed him the right glass. She'd known his suspicious ass would demand the right-hand glass if she offered the left. And Bob had played into her reverse psychology effortlessly.

THUD. Bob staggered and hit the floor.

Eva dragged Bob towards the door. Monica quickly retreated back to her car. She switched on the quiet engine, switched off the headlights, and slowly reversed until she was a few meters away from the house. Monica couldn't afford to be seen. She needed to know what was going on, but she now feared for her life. Not only was her best friend a home wrecker, but she was also a criminal.

Eva dragged Bob out of the house. Monica watched from a distance as she lifted Bob into the trunk of her car. *How did she get so strong?*

Eva turned the ignition on, and the car pulled out. Monica waited a bit before following behind. Thankfully, her friend didn't speed off like she normally did. She was rather calm, collected, and calculated in her driving.

After about 30 minutes, the scenery and landscape became familiar. Monica thought they were headed to her cabin in the woods. With this in mind, Monica maintained a safe distance. Moments later, the cabin came into view. On the left was a hilly, untarred, and dusty road. The cabin sat just in front of the road's end, with many corners and hideouts. It was a proper getaway destination.

Monica watched Erica park her car a short distance from her cabin. She then parked about a quarter of a mile away in a secluded corner to avoid any detection and walked stealthily towards the cabin. On arrival, she saw Erica standing over two bodies situated a fair distance from the cabin.

Monica observed closely. "Aubrey!" she exclaimed in a frightened whisper, covering her mouth. At least, the body of the woman's outfit matched what she'd seen Aubrey wearing the last time she'd seen her. Monica was distraught. For the second time that night, devastating news had wrought irreparable emotional damage.

Consumed by panic, Monica did all she could to conceal her muffled whimpering at the sight of her friend's body. Terror gripping her, she lost balance, slipping on her own feet. *Clank, clank, clank.* She quickly regained balance, but not before accidentally kicking a metal pail nearby. Erica immediately turned to her with full aggression.

"Who's there?!" she shouted, aggressively making her way towards the sound, but a sudden rush of wind halted her. She paused, judging the wind to be the cause of the noise. She turned and walked back.

Terrified, Monica quickly attempted to hide. Not finding anywhere suitable, she tried the front door. It didn't budge. She quickly rushed towards the back. On the first attempt, the door opened, so she crept in.

Monica almost vomited at the unbearable stench inside. It was dark, cold, and wet. Monica tiptoed to the front window, observing Erica while trying to use her cell phone to dial for help. "Crap! No reception! Of all times! Damn it!"

Monica's movements had alerted the real Erica down in the basement. Erica knew it was someone other than Eva because Eva's routine was distinct and never changed: she drove in and made her way straight down to the basement to update her on how much damage she'd wrought in her life for the week, and to continue her crazy show with the dolls. This was how she had learned of Monica's pregnancy and Eva's escapades with Anthony.

Instinctively, Erica began making as much noise as she could. Monica heard the muffled sounds. She calmed her breathing to be sure. The sounds were coming from the basement. Cautiously, Monica made her way towards the basement, her heart in her mouth.

More than halfway down the stairs with enough light shining from above to see somewhat, Monica stopped in her tracks the moment she saw another Erica. It all made sense now. She looked Erica up and down. The resemblance was uncanny. *How is this possible? Who is the woman outside? A doppelgänger?*

Erica was covered with bruises and bleeding from her face and several other regions. Erica wriggled her head, forcing Monica out of her shock and into action to quickly remove the duct tape.

"Oh, Monica! Thank God it's you," Erica began crying. She paused for a moment to collect her breath, then continued, "She killed Aubrey, Monica. That evil, crazy bitch killed Aubrey. I'm so sorry, Monica. I'm so sorry about Anthony!" Erica was now sobbing uncontrollably.

"Shhh." Monica said, placing her index finger on Erica's lips and hugging her along with the pole she was tied to. The evil doppelgänger had tied her up vindictively. It didn't even make sense the way she was tied up. "We need to get you out of here fast. We can worry about all of that later," Monica consoled her.

Monica began to untie Erica but stopped when the door upstairs banged open. Eva had entered the cabin and was now making her way straight down to the basement, as was her routine.

"Bitch! I'm home!" Eva shouted from upstairs; she then stepped loudly downstairs towards the basement.

"Quick, quick, Monica, hide," Erica urgently mentioned.

Monica was no longer overwhelmed by panic. Seeing Erica, the real one, she now had a better grip on her emotions. She gently, without any noise, hid behind a dryer. It helped that the basement was full of stuff, thanks to Erica's compulsive shopping habits.

"Hello, sis. Let me tell you a secret," Eva began, laughing callously. "I sent Monica an anniversary present. I recorded Anthony while he was working me up really good the other day, and I sent the video to Monica's house with instructions. I timed the delivery perfectly, and it got to the party right in time to throw a big damper on that façade of a party of theirs."

Erica was unresponsive. Monica's appearance had ushered in so much hope and her friend just needed to bide her time and remain hidden until Eva's departure.

Annoyed at her unresponsiveness, Eva slapped her again and again. She winced in pain.

"ENOUGH!" Erica screamed. "Okay! You've had your revenge, even though I don't know what I did to you. Come on, Eva, just let me go. I will pay you whatever you want. I promise. And I won't tell the police about any of this."

Eva interjected with mocking laughter. "I already have access to all your money, sis. I went into your bank and withdrew your money from your account and reported that your debit and credit cards were lost so I can get new ones shipped to the house then I added my own pin number. And as for the cops, they don't like you. Let's not even begin talking about your friends. You're probably the most hated person in Georgia right now. And oh! As for what you did to me? Good question with a simple answer: she chose you. That stupid woman chose you."

"What are you …? I don't …" Erica sat up with a confused expression. "Who are you talking about?"

"Mom, you idiot! Mom chose you. That bitch sold me, then gave you a life I could only dream about," Eva shouted, infuriated. She was now boiling over in anger and recounted her entire life experience up until this point. "Why you, and why me? Why weren't you the one sold? Why was I the one sold? The reasons don't even matter at this point. Now, I'm going to make both of you pay."

Erica felt guilty. She couldn't imagine what life must have been like for her sister. And what's more, she couldn't imagine how she would have felt after she found out she'd been rejected. She felt a pang of sadness; her sister had lived her whole life as the rejected twin. Regardless, Eva wasn't right upstairs, and bargaining with her was a complete waste of time.

Eva turned to leave, having updated Erica on the details of all her escapades. With two steps in, she turned and continued, "Before I forget, we'll be having a family reunion soon. I already have Mom's address, and I'm going for her next."

"Eva! You better leave her alone," Erica shouted, pissed.

Eva didn't respond, she just continued walking lackadaisically.

"You hear me?! You better leave—"

Erica's voice was cut off by the banging of the basement door. Eva continued outside in a cartoonish dance, doused in elation with the seamless execution of her plan. She paused momentarily, deeply inhaling the smell of burning bodies, basking in the euphoria of continuous victory. Content with the experience, she entered Erica's car and zoomed off.

The screech of the tires and rush of the car's engine as it left meant the coast was clear. Monica climbed out from behind the dryer, quickly untied Erica, and helped her up.

*****

"Excuse me, nurse, can you locate my mother?"

"Sure, ma'am, what's her name?" the nurse receptionist politely responded.

"Helen Jackson." Erica provided the additional information requested, hoping Eva hadn't gotten to her yet.

The nurse looked up from the computer monitor. "It looks like she has already been discharged, ma'am."

"What do you mean, she's been discharged?" Erica questioned the nurse. "Are you sure? Please check again."

"Ma'am, according to our system, she was discharged about 20 minutes ago. She left with her daughter, Erica Jackson," the nurse finished.

Erica leaned her frail frame into Monica. "It's Eva, Monica! She got here before us. Oh, God! Where could she be? Erica, think, think!" Erica said, pacing in frustration.

Eva had taken full advantage of her twinship with Erica. Ideally, a discharge could only be processed by the person who committed the patient. They wouldn't have discharged Helen otherwise. A surge of adrenaline and reality had fully come into view. Her memory clicked, and reasoning provided a location.

"Call the police," Erica demanded. "She talked about a family reunion, remember? I think she is taking Mom back to the cabin. She doesn't know I've escaped," Erica concluded.

Monica dialed 911 on the way. After Erica's brief explanation of what was going on and why they needed help, a dial tone followed, and the phone disconnected.

Monica and Erica were welcomed to the cabin by a note that read, "If you want her alive, come to 11352 NW Madison alone."

"That's my house," Erica said.

"This bitch is really crazy," Monica added.

As quickly as they got out of the car, they got back in, speeding off. Monica wanted to call Anthony but kept going back and forth with herself over it. Eventually, she took out her phone and dialed him. She explained everything, and before he hung up, he promised to go to Erica's.

Erica and Monica approached Erica's home cautiously when they arrived. Erica's car wasn't in sight, but the front door was ajar. Erica had a simple and straightforward plan: retrieve her Glock 45 from the kitchen cabinet. Erica slowly opened the door and made her way in. Monica followed behind her.

"Wait here. Let me get my gun. It's in the kitchen cabinet," Erica beckoned to Monica.

"Okay," Monica obliged.

Erica crouched down, stealthily making her way towards the counter. Suddenly, Erica heard a loud thudding sound and turned, but she was knocked out before seeing who it was.

CHAPTER 12
False Hope

"Erica. Erica."

Erica could hear her name being called. But it seemed to echo like it was coming from a distance. She tossed and turned till her eyes eventually opened. Everything was a blur at first, but within moments, her vision became clearer. The doctor looked at her with curiosity boldly plastered on his face, and she could tell he'd been the one calling.

The memory of getting shot played through her mind as the doctor examined her with a touch. She immediately jerked up in reaction.

"Woah! Relax! You've been in a coma for some time now. Your reflexes will gradually return to you, but for now, just take it easy."

As the doctor concluded and left, her mind reverted to Eva. She'd woken up tied to the same pole in the basement of the cabin after she was knocked out. Only this time, Monica and her mom, Helen, were tied up alongside her. She'd pleaded for Monica's release, but Eva wouldn't budge.

Eva then turned to their mom, screaming, "This is what it feels like to lose your whole world," while pointing Erica's Glock 45 at her. In between Helen's scream and Eva's mad ranting, Erica lost consciousness as blood trickled from her head due to the gunshot wound Eva inflicted. *The irony of being shot by your own gun.*

Knock, knock.

A knock on the door interrupted Erica's thoughts. She was met by Anthony's welcoming face. Tears began to fall from her eyes. Anthony rushed and hugged her, kissing her forehead.

"I rushed here as soon as I heard you were awake," Anthony said.

Erica tried speaking but was interrupted by profuse coughing.

"Take your time. Take your time," he admonished her.

"What happened?" Erica asked with a curious and worried expression.

"Well, after Monica called me, I rushed to your house. No one was there; just a blood trail that led from the house to what looked like where the car was parked. The blood trail suggested two people were bleeding. The way they were side by side to each other, it suggested the two of them were carried at the same time," Anthony explained. "I got through to some of my connections in the police department and we began looking for y'all. We eventually found that she'd taken y'all to your cabin in the woods. My police friend searched for your name Erica to see if you owned other properties and bingo you did. By the time we got there, thankfully early enough, both you and your mother were out cold. Long story short, your mom died three days after the incident, and you've been in a coma for six months."

Erica closed her eyes in pain, tears running down her face uncontrollably. Her mom had been such an important aspect of her life. They had been through the toughest times together. Although she felt deeply for Eva, her mom didn't deserve to die this way.

"Where is Monica?" Erica continued, tears still profusely running down her cheeks.

"She's still missing. And the baby should have been born by now," he said somberly.

"Get me out of here; we are going to go find them."

"Rest. You can't even walk, so you're in no shape to be looking for someone. The police and I are still searching; we have pictures of Monica constantly on the news, in newspapers, and on flyers. She will come up," he assured her.

"I'll tell you this: I might not have known or grown up with her, but I feel my sister's pain, and I see visions of her. That pain is so strong and now it's driven by rage. I'm so afraid of what she'll do next." She looked at Anthony intensely. "Listen to me, she is going to keep Monica alive because she wanted that baby, but once it's born, she has no more use for Monica. You must find her now."

Immediately, Erica became dizzy. She was met by quick flashes of images. She shrieked in pain.

"Hey, Erica! Are you okay? What happened?" Anthony inquired, deeply concerned by her sudden acute change in mental status.

"Quick, Anthony. I know where they are, and Monica is in grave danger. Call it a premonition or whatever, but I just saw a vision of their whereabouts."

It was an abandoned farmhouse by a lake. It had a reddish brick look on the outside and an old window with chipped paint. Woods surrounded it and there was a school up the road with a red, white, and blue flag hanging from the window. The farmhouse was in Kansas City, Missouri. It was Eva and Erica's mother's maternal home. She'd been taken there when she was very little.

Anthony took the details and reached out to his connections in the police department, and they sprang into action. Within five days, they'd recovered Eva and Monica with no hassle. Eva hadn't seen it coming. Monica was admitted to the same hospital as Erica for observation, being already far along in the pregnancy. Eva was admitted into the same mental institution her mom was in before she'd killed her.

CHAPTER 13
New Beginning Cut Short

A week later, Erica was chilling, sunbathing, and listening to some good music. Everything was back on track. She was healing rapidly and had regained all her motor abilities. Monica was also okay, and she and Anthony were in the process of reconciling. Erica was staying with the couple in the meantime until she was completely sorted out.

Mr. Wang, the CEO at her job, had called, offering her job back with heavy bonuses and retro payments dating back to when they thought she was dead until they received the good news of her survival. Several news channels had requested interviews for her to tell her story, and the police were offering to pay damages. It seemed God was beginning to hand down a smile.

The incessant ringing of the phone finally caught her attention. Erica quickly turned down the stereo and picked up the call, as it had been ringing for a while.

"Hello?" Erica began. But there wasn't any response. The caller just kept breathing deep into the phone, sending waves of shivers down Erica's spine. In a panicked voice, Erica asked again, "Who the hell is this?!"

"I'm coming for you, sis!" Eva calmly said, then let out an evil laugh. "I'm coming for you, Anthony, and Monica! I'm coming for you all!" Eva finished and dropped the call.

It was a private number. Erica immediately called out to Monica, prompting a quick response of Anthony. Monica, who had been in the kitchen, sluggishly, as fast as her legs could carry her big belly, joined them by the pool. In an unplanned chorus, Monica and Anthony asked, "What is it?"

"It's Eva! She's escaped!"

POWERTALK RESOURCE PAGE

I hope you enjoyed the book! Even though the characters are fictional, people all over the world suffer from mental illness, molestation, and abandonment. This PowerTalk Resource page is a guide to help individuals who are searching for support. Please know you are not alone and that there's help to assist you in your time of need.

Suicide Mental Health

National Suicide Prevention Hotline
1-800-273-8255 available 24/7

National Alliance on Mental Health Issues
1-800-950-6264 Mon-Fri 10 a.m. – 10 p.m. EST

Sexual/Domestic Child Abuse

National Domestic Violence Hotline
1-800-799-7233 and online chat available 24/7

National Child Abuse Hotline
1-800-422-4453 available 24/7

Rape, Abuse, and Incest National Network
1-800-656-4673

American Oversees Domestic Violence Crisis Center
First, find your AT&T USA Direct access code (available online). Then dial the AT&T USA Direct access code for the country you are currently in at the prompt, enter the phone number **866-879-6636**

Addiction/Drug Abuse

Substance Abuse and Mental Health Services
1-800-663-4357 available 24/7

Cocaine Hotline
1-800-262-2463

Health

Aids National Hotline
1-800-621-4000

STD Hotline
1-800-227-8922

National Center for HIV/AIDS, Viral Hepatitis, STDs & TB Prevention
1-800-232-4636

ABOUT THE AUTHOR

Lynell is an entrepreneur, author, Certified Life Coach, and educator. She was born and raised in the City of Brotherly Love, Philadelphia, Pennsylvania, which is also where she earned her bachelor's degree in Business Management from Strayer University. She excelled in her collegiate studies, becoming president of the National Honor Society of Collegiate Scholars for adult students nationwide. She was also elected to the Student Advisory Board and created a business club for beginner entrepreneurs on campus. As a career-driven single mother of two boys, she has endured many struggles. At a young age, she began writing to cope with her challenges. Writing children's mini-stories, poetry, and suspense literature became a way to express her emotions and release stress.

Lynell is the Founder of Helping Other People In Need (HOP-IN2), a non-profit 501(c)3 organization. As a community liaison, her goal was to design a program that supports individuals and their families who suffer from trauma and grief due to the loss of a loved one to street violence and/or injustice. The passion and love she has for helping people empowered her to open Allegiant Assistant Home Care, a healthcare agency that provides non-medical and transportation services to disabled children, adults, and seniors. She hopes her literature, activism, and legacy will be a gift she gives to the world that will last an eternity.

If you would like to read more or be a part of Helping Other People In Need, please go to www.hopin2.org or email lynellsmith@lynellbookstore.com. Together we can change lives one person at a time.

SHOP WITH US

As an entrepreneur myself, I like to showcase and highlight other businesses and entrepreneurs on my platforms. To have your business featured in one of my upcoming projects, please send the name of your business, your contact information, and why you would like to be featured. Using the subject "Entrepreneur Highlight," send an email to: lynellsmith@lynellbookstore.com

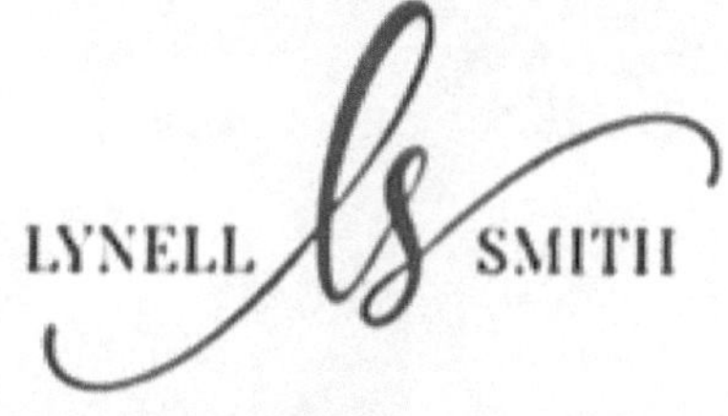

Specializing in things that authors love, the bookstore showcases a variety of reading materials, mugs, and other pleasantries that make author and reader life wonderful! For more information, click the logo, or visit: www.lynellbookstore.com

Specializing in sporty casual wear, Something Light's slogan is simple, "something light, nothing heavy." Everything doesn't have to be so hard, tread lightly, take it easy and let things flow. It's more than just a concept and an idea, it's a way of living. Think of us as a fresh brand for the everyday independent man/woman. For more information, click the hat to the left or visit: www.somethinglightclothing.com

Birthed from a childhood memory and dream, Hashawn Carey is a casual luxury apparel brand. Hashawn Carey offers inspired looks for men and women and specializes in customer experience and service. To see for yourself, click the logo, or visit: www.hashawncarey.com